# Yeval

# Yeval

C.W. Schultz

2007

# Yeval

*To my family for their undying love and support. Also to my friends for the good times past, present and future.*

CHAPTER I

# Brother

I'M IN NEED OF THERAPY. This is why I have an appointment to see Dr. Baker at 4:30 this afternoon.

I'm dumping off my kid brother, Ryan, at Maple Way Residence, home for the disabled. Ryan, my only sibling, is my best friend. He is nine years my junior and is mentally-retarded. There was an accident when my mother was pregnant with him, resulting in her death and Ryan's three month premature birth. My father put him in Maple Way Residence about three years ago. To my surprise, it was actually best for Ryan. He used to do nothing all day except watch television and walk circles around the living room. Now, living in a home, he has made friends with other goofballs. He even has a girlfriend. The people who take care of him are really nice, too. They cook for him and do his laundry. Once a week the residents have a field trip to either the ball-game or a movie.

Today is Thursday. Thursday is the day Ryan and I spend together. Always. Unfortunately, Yeval taunted me about Mother's death again last night, so I scheduled an emergency appointment with Dr. Baker. Thankfully, I was available to take Ryan out to lunch so we could enjoy at least a few hours of each other's company. Spending time with my brother comforts me; his presence is a reminder of our childhood.

I pull up to the front entrance of the complex in my 2007 Chrysler Sebring. Ryan smiles at me and remains buckled in the passenger's seat. I smile back, knowing that he doesn't want to leave. We sit in silence. As the seconds go by, I feel more and more guilty about cutting our day short.

"I wish we could've hung out longer, but my doctor only works afternoons," I lie. "She's very busy, so I can't reschedule."

I don't want Ryan to know that I've been in therapy. He thinks I'm just going in for a checkup.

"Okay. It was fun. We need to hang out for longer again," he says, trying to be positive.

"What are you doing tomorrow?"

"Field trip."

"Oh yeah," I remember. "Cool. That sounds fun."

"Dad wants to get together on Saturday. You want to come with us?"

"I'd like that, but—you know how Dad is." I'm trying to be polite; the thought of my father angers me.

"Are you two still fighting?" my brother asks. Ryan knows me too well.

"No," I snap. "We have nothing to fight about. I'm my own man and he's *his* own man. We shouldn't be telling each other what to do."

I shake my head.

"He just doesn't approve of my lifestyle," I say, trying to justify my sudden anger.

"Oh," Ryan says, slightly uncomfortable. "Right."

"And I don't approve of the way he judges me."

I want to change the subject.

"Nora still tells me what to do, and I'm twenty," Ryan says as he fidgets with his seatbelt.

Nora is the one who usually takes care of Ryan. She is a stubby little Mexican lady, probably in her early forties. She is an absolute saint every time I see her, but what's this I hear about her telling my brother what to do?

"Do you like Nora? Is she taking good care of you?" I ask, genuinely concerned.

"Yeah. She's good. I like Nora, she's nice. I'm glad she's here."

"Do you like it here, Ryan?"

"People like me are here. I feel like normal. This is where I want to be," he says insistently.

"Okay. Just checking. I want you to let me know if there's ever a problem."

Ryan nods, almost as though he doesn't really care about what I just said. Am I being overprotective?

"You're my little brother and I want you living in a comfortable place."

"I don't need a babysitter," he says, annoyed. "Like you said, I'm my own man."

Okay, now I know I'm being overly protective. I try to redeem myself by saying, "Hey, you're my brother. Whatever concerns you concerns me. You got that? I hope you think the same way for me."

"Uh-huh."

It's 4:10 now. It takes me exactly twenty minutes to get from Maple Way to Dr. Baker's. I know this because I've timed the journey several times. I time myself quite often; I like to arrive exactly on time. Arriving late is just plain rude, while arriving early takes up your own time because you usually end up waiting. I don't want to waste a second of my life—I have already wasted too much of my time obsessing about not wasting time. Now *that's* what you call contradictory.

Yeah, I need major help.

"Well, I'll see you later," I say, feeling like a bigger asshole by rushing the goodbye.

"Yup. So, I'll see you Saturday?" he asks, knowing I don't want to see my father.

"Yeah, sure," I confirm, rolling my eyes. I can't say no because Ryan will think I'm an even bigger asshole for purposely avoiding my father. "I'm going to call up Dad first. But expect me there and I'll call you if I can't," I put in, just in case I change my mind.

"Okay. See ya, dude," he says, opening the door.

"Later bro," I say, as he closes the door.

I watch to make sure he gets in the house okay. He walks up the stairs, past a resident on the porch swing, and enters the building.

Okay. Back to my fucked up life.

CHAPTER 2

# Doctor

It's in the waiting area of room 304, on the third floor of the John Fern Building, that I notice a receptionist I've never seen before. She has long brown hair, dark-brown eyes, milky skin and perfectly shaped breasts. The first thing I think when I see her, which is probably what most guys think, is how much I'd like to fuck her. She's sitting down behind her desk, so I can't see her ass. Judging from her appearance, I'm sure she has an ass I'd like to fuck as well.

I walk up to her desk to check in. I approach her with a smile, showing off my snow-white teeth that are actually oversized, but what can you do?

"Good afternoon. Randy Mulray here to see Dr. Baker."

I peek at my watch; it's 4:29. I can be so smooth when I want to be.

"At 4:30," I quickly add, with a sly chuckle and a handsomely wide smirk.

"I'm sorry, but Dr. Baker isn't here," she tries to say politely. She smiles, letting me know that she finds me attractive.

"Nonsense," I say, meek but cool. "Dr. Baker set up an appointment with me yesterday. She's in room 304B."

"I'm sorry, but Dr. Baker is not in," she replies, still smiling at me.

It's unusual for Dr. Baker to flake out on me, especially when it's a crisis.

I'm about to panic. Thoughts begin to race. I feel like the world will end if I don't talk to Dr. Baker.

"Hmm. That's strange. Well, is she available tomorrow?"

"I'm sorry, but Dr. Baker won't be in for a while," she answers, still smiling.

I look around to make sure I'm in 304. I am. Something weird is going on and I'm already beyond the point of agitation.

"This must be some kind of mistake. Dr. Baker never forgets. She's supposed to be here to talk with me," I point out, trying really hard not to show how upset I have suddenly become.

"Yeah, I know," she says, *still* fucking smiling! "They don't tell me anything, I'm just a receptionist. But what I heard is that something has come up."

I feel like slamming both of my fists down on her desk to startle her. Then I'd like to scream in her face, so close that she can feel the warmth of my breath, "Get me Dr. Baker you fucking ugly cunt!" I'd like to see her stupid smile drop and her face blush in fear. She looks like a girl who might start crying if someone yells at her. If I were to do this, then maybe it'll register in her pretty little head that life is only a breeze for her because she is gorgeous. But I don't say anything. Instead, I'm interrupted by some guy in his mid-fifties.

"Are you Randy Mulray?" he asks.

"Yes," I respond suspiciously.

"I'm Dr. Dwight Jenkins."

He puts his hand out and I shake it.

Dr. Jenkins smiles at me and walks over to Dr. Baker's office. He unlocks the door and tells me to come in.

I enter, glancing over my shoulder at the receptionist. I catch her looking me up and down. I give her a death stare, letting her know that I'm not into her. For some reason, this satisfies me.

Dr. Jenkins closes the door behind us and takes a seat at Dr. Baker's desk. What the fuck is going on?

"What the fuck is going on?" I decide to say out loud.

Dr. Jenkins is surprised at my language.

I apologize for my foul mouth.

He tells me to take a seat, so I do.

"Randy, I'm afraid I have some bad news."

I wonder what it could be? Is Dr. Baker sick? Out of town?

"Dr. Baker was in a car accident last night," he tells me. "She didn't make it."

"Why wasn't I notified earlier?" I immediately ask. No emotion or understanding has sunk in yet.

"We just found out."

I sit on Dr. Baker's cozy couch, purposely frozen. I'm not sure what feelings I want to show to this guy, calling himself Dr. Jenkins. I'm feeling angrier, more depressed, more hopeless and more confused than I did earlier. Whatever feelings I want to hide, sadness can't be one of them. My throat hardens and my sight blurs.

"Do you want to discuss your feelings?" he asks softly.

"What is there to talk about?" I say, wiping a tear from my cheek. "She's gone and she's not coming back."

Dr. Jenkins opens his mouth, about to say something when I interrupt, "She was a smart and caring person who dedicated her life to helping others. She was taken too soon. She could've helped more people. She could've helped me! She *was* helping me."

Jenkins holds back a smile; my little blabber amused him. My God, I've turned into such a drama-queen.

I put my head in my palms and begin sobbing quietly. It's better I get it out of my system as soon as possible. I don't want to bottle this shit and have Yeval find out and make things ten times worse.

Minutes pass. Dr. Jenkins lets me get myself together. When I finally calm down, I look back up at him, noticing that he's staring at me.

"I was given Dr. Baker's notes. I can help you."

I want to tell this stranger that he doesn't know me, he can't ask for the relationship I built with Dr. Baker, and that he can't expect me to have the energy to start my therapy from scratch. But I keep my mouth shut because this stranger is trying to help me and I appreciate it.

"What should I do? I have to start all over again."

Dr. Jenkins spends the next ten minutes trying to convince me to stay and pick up where Dr. Baker and I left off. I make it clear that I don't want to open up to somebody I don't know. But Dr. Jenkins still doesn't give up. I admire that. Finally, he tricks me into a discussion when he asks, "Why don't you tell me why you think you need therapy?"

"Read Dr. Baker's notes."

"I prefer to have you explain it to me. In your own words."

"I see things," I answer, intentionally vague.

Dr. Jenkins opens the file, skimming. Is he trying to find an answer? He flips through it as if he already read it, which he probably has. But he suddenly pauses and sees something he apparently didn't notice before.

"Yeval," he says, though I can't tell if he's just saying Yeval or if he's asking me about Yeval. So I don't respond. He looks up from the file and says, "Tell me about Yeval."

"Yeval is a creature I see from time to time."

"Is he a friend?"

"No, he is just a creature that I see from time to time." I'm irritated now.

"Does Yeval talk to you?"

"Sometimes."

"What does he say?"

"He explains to me why I'm a bad person. Yeval thinks it's because of me that my mother is dead. He says I killed her. Yeval says it's my fault my brother is retarded too."

"Do you believe that? You were only nine when your mother died."

I'm too overwhelmed at the moment to try and explain something this deep and personal to someone who doesn't even know me.

"I don't want to talk about it."

"That's okay. We can talk about something else. Do you have a job?"

"No."

"How do you get by?"

"I'm an independent salesman."

"Drugs?" he asks, although I'm positive he already knows this from the file. "Does your brother know?" he asks.

I tell Jenkins that my brother doesn't know, which is the truth. Ryan probably doesn't even know what marijuana is.

"Your father?"

"Yes, my father knows."

"Is that the main reason you two don't get along?"

"What makes you think I don't get along with my father?"

"Do you get along with your father?"

I want to say that I do get along with my father, just to make Dr. Know-it-all feel a little less sure of himself. But lying just doesn't seem right—I'm trying to make progress here. Instead, I tell Dr. Jenkins that I want to go home.

"You're right," he says. "I'm being too forward. I'm sorry."

I stand up and head towards the door. I think for a minute then decide to set my check on the desk. Dr. Jenkins takes the check and gives it back to me.

"This appointment is free."

"Oh. Good."

I kind of snatch the check back.

"Listen. I really want to help you. I know I can't take Dr. Baker's place, but I'm still here for you. I can help you. It may be too soon for you to understand that, but I'm willing to help you if you're willing to return."

Even though I find his words a bit clichéd, they comfort me. It's in his voice that I sense he's sincerity.

"Thank you," I nod.

"Would you be willing to come back on Monday?"

He's worried about me. I can tell.

I accept, though I'm not sure I want to come back. But if I don't want to, I can always cancel or just not show up.

He shakes my hand and wishes me a good weekend, then gives me his home phone number just in case I need to talk with him immediately. What a nice guy.

I leave the room feeling a lot better than I did coming in, even though I didn't really make any progress. I'm pleased that this stranger who calls himself Dr. Jenkins helped me feel a little less depressed about everything, including Dr. Baker's death.

I wonder if he really can help. The thought excites me. Could this Dr. Jenkins be a new beginning for me?

CHAPTER 3

# Home

The odor from Morgan's cigarettes coming from my apartment is so strong I can smell them before I even enter my goddamn room. I told her a hundred times not to smoke in the room.

I unlock the door and walk into my cozy apartment that reeks because Morgan, my girlfriend (if that's what you want to call her) chain-smokes whenever I'm gone. I'm always confronting her about how she doesn't do anything useful and how she doesn't abide by *my* rules in *my* apartment. Inevitably, she argues back with something completely unrelated. Today, I'm not in the mood.

I close the front door and walk into the living room where Morgan is playing a video-game. Since when did she start playing video-games?

A cigarette is pressed between her lips. She hits pause every twenty seconds to ash the cancer in an empty soda can. It's better than on the table.

Morgan is about six foot, but weighs 130 pounds. She is an eighth Thai (from her great-grandmother, I think) and the rest of her is pure white-trash. Her skin is white, but she's got these stunning slanted hazel eyes, proving she's not one-hundred-percent trailer-honky. Right now they're red, which leads me to believe she's stoned on my supply. This angers me even more than her cigarette smoking.

Morgan wears a white tank top, so tight that her ridiculously oversized tits are about to pop out. It's the same tank top she was wearing when I left, telling me that she hasn't done shit all day. I don't know how she keeps her perfect body when she does nothing with her life but eat, sleep, fuck, smoke, snort, fuck some more, suck and fuck even more.

I sometimes wonder if Morgan is the most useless person on the planet. She doesn't really even live here. It was about a year ago when I gave into my temptation and had a one night stand with her. Ever since, we've been fucking more and more often. I guess this established a boyfriend/

girlfriend thing. I've come to be okay with this, but would it kill her to help out around the joint once in a while—buy some food, pay part of the rent? After all, she eats most of the food and is in this apartment more than me.

"Hey honey." I try to sound affectionate.

"Hey you."

I want to talk more but have nothing to say. Neither does she. Kind of embarrassing actually. I play this off as just a simple greeting and walk into the kitchen. I pour myself a bowl of Apple Jacks. After opening the refrigerator, I notice Morgan drank all the milk again. I sigh in a mixture of disappointment and frustration.

"I'm gong to the store, I'll be back in a few. You need anything?" I shout from the kitchen.

"Yeah," she says, walking into the kitchen, still smoking that fucking cigarette. "I need you. I need my fix."

Oh no, she's cranky. I can tell that she smoked the rest of my stash and that I probably won't be getting any pussy tonight.

"You left me at home all day," she continues.

*You didn't have to stay at home, bitch.*

She continues, "Then you come home for two seconds and you're about to leave again!"

"You drank all the milk, girl," I say defensively. "I gotta buy some more."

She should be buying more milk, not me. Bitch.

"You spend more time with your retarded brother than you do with me."

I notice that her cigarette is gone. Where the fuck did she put it out?

"What did you just say?" I ask, trying to be intimidating. I usually do a great job of intimidating people, but I know it won't work on Morgan because she's been with guys who would actually abuse her. She knows I'd never hurt her and the slut takes advantage of that.

"I said your brother is retarded," she answers, even though I wasn't really asking her to repeat what she had just said.

Right now I wish I could slap her upside her pretty hollow head and say, "It was a rhetorical question, you no good skank." Instead, I pussy out and say, "You're so close to being homeless, girl. I do everything around here. Literally. So, remember your place before you go insulting my family."

The bitch doesn't say anything.

I open the counter-drawer, second from the top, where I keep my scale, weed, Swishers, and 'shrooms or ecstasy if I'm in stock. I only carry mushrooms and ecstasy when it's in high demand—no harder drugs. I always try to have weed in stock. When I look in the drawer, I notice that all the pot has been smoked. But Morgan also indulged in all my Swishers.

"The Swishers too, Morgan?" I say, in a tone that lets her know I'm disappointed in her. I don't think she could care less. I continue, "You're useless. Please don't smoke my shit anymore. The more you smoke the less I have to sell." She starts to say something, when I interrupt, "Meaning the less money I have to pay for your broke ass." Ha! That was cool. Now I'm winning the argument for sure.

"Let me tell you something, *Randy*," she says, enunciating my name (something my father likes to do). "When you run out of your shit, I'll run out on you. There are plenty of other guys who want me."

I'm about to say the greatest come-back, pointing out that I'm already aware of that and that the only thing she is good for is sex. But I'm interrupted by a scratchy low voice from behind me that says, "She's right." It's Yeval.

"I don't want to talk to you right now," I say to him, without turning around to look at him.

"Fine. I'm going out for a while," says Morgan, thinking that I'm talking to her. She exits the kitchen, grabs her purse from the living room, and leaves the apartment, slamming the front door loudly as she goes.

"What are you fighting about this time?" Yeval asks.

"I told you I don't want to talk right now," I say leaving the kitchen, still not looking at him.

I walk into my bedroom. Morgan trashed it. Her clothes and shit are everywhere. I'll have to clean it up later. I feel like writing, so I take a seat at my desk where my laptop sits. I open it up, start Word Processor, double-space the format, put a header in the right-corner, set the font to Courier New size 12, and type, "Unicorns are galloping through fields of golden grass. Young Alexander watches them on a branch of the tall tree known as Gahlandtre. The yellow sun sinks, turning the sky red. Soon, the cool summer moon will rise." It takes me forty-two minutes to write this. I blame it on Yeval who distracts me by clicking his long yellow fingernails, one at a time, against the arm of a wooden chair he's sitting on in the corner.

"What!?" I yell at him, spinning my chair around to look at him.

He doesn't stop clicking his fingernails. He just smiles at me with his green razor-sharp shark teeth, staring back at me with the orange eyes of a cat.

"I'm sorry to hear about Dr. Baker," he says. Then he chuckles and the inner parts of his eyebrows lower as the outer part of them rise.

"What do you want, Yeval?" I ask him as I turn back around to my computer. "Anything new? Or are you just here to taunt me as usual?"

Yeval has always appeared at the worst possible times to taunt me about what a bad person I am. Whether that's because I'm a drug dealer, how I don't really "love" my "girlfriend", how it's my fault my brother is retarded, how it's my fault my mother is dead, how it's my fault my father is a widower, how it's my fault Caroline broke up with me, or just something as simple as me being stupid.

Yeval is a demonic creature that shows up a few times a day. He has heartless eyes with pencil-thin vertical pupils, dirty-green razor-sharp triangular teeth, pointed elf ears, and cherry-red skin. Yeval is about five and a half feet tall, and very skinny. He's very human like as he has all the limbs we do and stands in a bipedal manner, but moves quickly and sneakily like a crab.

Yeval has been with me since I was nine. This year marks twenty years of living with him. Today, I expect him to make me feel like Dr. Baker's death was my fault.

"I have something to show you," he says.

"I don't want to see it," I say.

I hear the high-pitched ring of a triangle. I turn around to see what it is.

A large pearl, about an inch and a half in diameter, floats between Yeval and me. I've never seen it before.

"Grab it and come with me into the Dark Room," he says.

Over the years Yeval has done nothing but talk and taunt. This is the first time he has ever had to "show" me something.

"Grab on to the Pearl and come with me into the Dark Room," he repeats.

The Pearl is so shiny and beautiful. It makes me wonder if Yeval has something beautiful to show me. I decide to take a hold of it so I know what it feels like and why it is floating.

I grab the Pearl in midair and examine it. Resting in my hands, I can tell it weighs at least a couple of pounds. How the hell can it float?

As it lays in my right hand, I run the fingers of my left hand over it. It's solid and smooth. Could it be valuable? It's so beautiful; I wish I had hundreds of these.

When I look up from my hand I notice I'm in a room. But it's not my room. It's a room I've never been in before. The floors and walls are all black, and appear to all be the same size. It's like I'm inside a cube.

There are two red chairs sitting together against one of the walls. A yellow curtain covers the entire side of the wall on the opposite side of the chairs. The other two walls both have one small window on each of them. There are no doors. How did I get in here? How do I get out?

I walk over to the window on the left side of the chairs. I look out and see a long dirt road that leads to hills. There is nothing between the hills and me except for a single burnt tree. The sky is dark, like night. No moon or stars are in view.

I walk over to the other window and look out. I see a field of long golden grass. It leads to tall snow-covered mountains; the sun shines between the mountains' peak as it sets. The sky is red. There are several trees, dark-green and healthy. From a distance I see horses—maybe unicorns—loping in the field. There's a woman watching them. She has thick black hair tied in a ponytail. She is tall and wears a polka-dotted orange dress. I squint, trying to make out who she is. She looks so familiar and when I finally recall, I am startled by Yeval.

"Welcome to the Dark Room, Randy," he says.

I turn my attention to Yeval who sits on the left chair.

"How did I get here?" I demand.

"You grabbed the Pearl."

"How do I get out of here?"

"Oh, but you just got here."

It's no use. Knowing Yeval, he's not going to try and help me get out. I have to find my own way out.

I try to open both windows to no avail. I begin to fluster. My forehead dampens with sweat and breathing becomes an effort. I'm desperate for escape. Instead of wondering why I am in here, all I think about is how to get out.

Standing by the left window (the one with a dirt road and a burnt

15

tree), I scan the Dark Room for something to break the windows with. I don't see anything so I try to break the window with my elbow. Yeval laughs at me as I hurt myself. It doesn't stop me from trying again. I try to punch the window open, knowing that the consequences of using my fist to break glass could be extremely agonizing, but I'm desperate and tough so I do it anyway.

I punch the window several times with my *strong* fist, but it still doesn't break.

"There's only two ways to get out of the Dark Room," Yeval says.

"Oh okay, you decide to inform me of that now," I say, still very flustered. "So, tell me."

"Come sit," he says, patting the other chair.

I sit down, giving Yeval what he wants. I expect to return to my room, but nothing happens.

"So, Yeval, how do I get out of this place?"

"You must watch," Yeval says, pointing at the yellow curtain in front of us.

The yellow curtain slowly slides open from the middle, much like at the movies. In fact, behind the yellow curtain is a screen.

"Watch," Yeval says. "It's about to start!"

The screen is all black. An image comes on the screen. It's an image of a one-story house at night. The point of view is from the backyard, I assume. The image moves closer to the house, telling me that I am looking through the eyes of someone else.

"So, what is this, Yeval?"

I am a bit nervous because I'm unsure of what I am about to see.

"Just watch," he tells me. "You are in the eyes of Slayer."

"Slayer" is on the patio of the house. He scans the back-end of the house from right to left. The scanning stops when he sees a window on the left side of the house. Slayer moves in for a closer look. He runs his gloved-hands over the screen covering the window. Slayer's head tips down to waist level. He's dressed in all black. From his pocket, Slayer removes a pair of scissors.

He begins cutting a small hole in the screen. When he's done he puts the scissors back in his pocket. Sticking his index finger in the small hole, the screen comes off the window. Slayer sets it quietly on the ground.

He looks up from the ground and I notice that the window is open about four inches. That's why he chose that particular window.

Slayer puts his left arm in the opening of the window, grabs a hold of the lock on the inside, unlocks it, and slides it open.

Slayer crawls through the window and into the house. His feet land on the sink. He steps onto the floor and scans the room. He exits the kitchen and enters the hall. To the left is the living room. To the right is what seems to be an endless hallway that leads to four different doors, two on each side of the wall. Slayer walks down the hallway and quietly opens the first door on the left, a closet with a vacuum, raincoats and lunchboxes. He turns to the first door on the right, already opened, and sees that it's the bathroom.

Slayer walks down the hall to the last two doors, open as well. The last door on the right is a bedroom. From the door, I see a king size bed against the wall, and nightstands on each side of the bed. Two people are in the bed sleeping, a man and a woman. The foot of the bed faces the doorway. There's an aluminum baseball bat leaning against the man's nightstand.

Slayer creeps in cautiously. He moves left along the wall, lurking closer to the man's side of the bed.

Slayer quietly picks up the bat. Standing right next to the man, he raises the bat in the air and strikes down on the man's head. There is a quick, but extremely haunting and painful scream.

"Jesus!," I exclaim.

Yeval laughs.

The woman switches on her desk lamp that sits on her nightstand. She turns around with her eyes half shut, not knowing what she's about to see.

"What's wrong, honey?" she says softly, half asleep.

She must be a deep sleeper.

Her half shut eyes open full when she sees the blood.

Through Slayer's eyes, it appears Slayer hit the bottom of the man's skull, breaking his neck. The man's head tilts upward, while his body lays flat. There are small amounts of blood coming out of his nose and right-ear. From what I see, he is dead.

"What are you showing me, Yeval?" I ask, revolted.

"Just watch," he tells me.

"I don't want to watch."

"You have to watch if you want to leave the Dark Room."

I look back at the screen and see the woman in shock, staring into the eyes of Slayer. She's off her bed, breathing deeply. Her mouth opens and closes in an attempt to scream, but nothing comes out.

Slayer smashes down on the man's face again. There is a splat sound when the bat hits the man's head, denting his face. The man's body twitches briefly before it lays still again. Blood pulses onto the bedding from the several gashes in his face. His eyes leak blood. Smashed brains dangle from his head as the blood soaks into his pillow.

The woman makes a shrieking sound and falls to the ground. She tries to pull herself together and run, but she's in too much shock, so she attempts to crawl away.

Slayer walks over to the other side of the bed where she writhes. Her face is damp with tears, mucus, and drool. She leans on her left arm, and raises her right arm. She raises her hand to his face, telling him to stop. She is breathing very deeply but manages to say, "Don't!"

Slayer raises the bat. The woman watches as the bat comes down to strike her in the middle of her face. She doesn't even attempt to get out of the way. Her body plunges to the ground, as she begins crying in pain, looking straight up at the ceiling. Her nose broken, she's choking on her teeth. She spits them out; they land on the ground, on her stomach, and one even gets in her eye.

Slayer laughs and drops the bat. He exits the room and walks into the adjacent one. There he sees a little bed, lit by a night-light. A child sits in the room crying silently.

I too begin to cry. "This is terrible, Yeval. Why are you showing me this."

Yeval laughs at me.

"It's not funny," I yell. "What are you showing me?"

Yeval does nothing but smile and point at the screen.

"I want to go home," I sob.

"You finish watching what I have to show you and then you can go home."

"Fuck you," I snivel.

"If you watch, you will go home. If you don't watch, you stay here until you do watch."

"This is hell."

"You ain't seen nothing."

I hesitate to look back at the screen, but build up the courage to do it.

I cry some more.

Now Slayer takes the child from his bed. The child is a little brunette boy, probably three years old. He claws at the back of Slayer's head. I hope the child somehow escapes, but I have this chilling feeling that that's not what follows.

Slayer carries the screaming child into the kitchen and sets him in a highchair. He walks over to the sink and opens the cupboard below.

Under the sink are various household cleaning products; Windex, White King bleach, and Ajax. Slayer takes the White King out, sets the container on the counter and grabs a glass from the dishwasher. Slayer fills the cup with the bleach. He walks back over to the child who is desperately trying to escape from his highchair.

"Drink it," Slayer says, handing the child the glass.

The child just stares at it.

"Do it!" Slayer yells.

The crying child takes the glass, looks at the liquid inside and takes a little taste of it.

I think to myself how much I'd like to see the face of this bastard that Yeval calls Slayer. I want to look into the eyes of someone this evil and try to figure out why they'd do something like this for no apparent reason.

The child spits out the bleach and begins to cry some more.

"Drink it!" Slayer screams at him.

The child shakes his head. Slayer snatches the cup from the child, shoves it in the child's mouth, and holds his nose shut so he can't breath. After the second gulp, his eyes rolls back. After two more gulps, vomit pours from his mouth, filling the glass. It drips down the boy's chin.

Slayer throws the glass on the ground and walks back down the hall. He sees the woman in the hallway, sobbing loudly. She stares into her son's bedroom, at his empty little bed, knowing something's happened. Slayer steps over her, neither of the two seem to notice each other, and he walks into the bedroom.

The walls, bed, and floor are all stained in blood. Blood-drops from the woman's face have created a path from the bed to where she lies; still conscious and in pain. Slayer picks up the bloody bat.

He continues to smash her head with the bat, this time from behind. Her face flies into the floor and stays there. Her head is cracked open, swollen. Blood spews from the cracks like water from a fire-hydrant. Slayer mashes her skull again, this time her head pops open and I can see her pureed brain. She isn't crying so I assume (and hope) she is dead. Slayer takes another thrust at her head, this time almost flattening it out. Broken skull and pieces of brain are scattered around her headless body.

Slayer leans over and dips his finger in what's left of her brain and wiggles it around until it's damp with blood. He proceeds into the bathroom where I finally get a look at this sicko through his reflection in the mirror.

He is wearing a black sweatshirt, black sweatpants and latex gloves. To my surprise, he isn't wearing a mask. His face is covered with white paint, his hair is too. It's as if he dipped his head in a bucket of the stuff. His face is so distorted by the bright paint, I probably couldn't identify the guy even if I knew him. All I can tell from looking at him is that he has wrinkles, so he is an older man. His hair is slicked back because of the wetness of the paint, so I can't tell what texture the hair is. The shape of his face assures me he is Caucasian. His cheeks are round, but I can't tell if he is fat.

He has brown eyes, looking into the mirror. It looks like he's looking at me. Chills run down my spine. The bastard smiles at himself. His teeth and the white of his eyes look very yellow, but that's because of how bright the paint is.

He wipes his blood-dipped finger on the mirror, attempting to write something. The blood isn't thick enough to make out or finish what he's attempting to write.

"Shit," he whines to himself, leaving the bathroom. He walks up to the woman lying in the hallway and grabs a hunk of her battered brain. He returns to the bathroom with her brains in his right hand and he dips his left index finger into it. He writes on the mirror, dipping his finger into her brain when the blood thins out.

On the mirror he has written, "SLAYER". He smiles at himself again proudly, then hits the lights off and exits.

Slayer stands over the woman's body, and looks into the bedroom, enjoying the chaos he has created. He laughs, and then heads for the kitchen. There, he sees that the child has expired. Vomit covers his body, and his swollen blue neck has tilted his head upright. Foam slowly drips from the child's lips. Slayer laughs some more and then vanishes into the dark night.

The screen fades to black, and the lights from the Dark Room fade. It is pitch black. I can literally hear my heart pounding in fear as I sit in the darkness, not able to see or hear anything. Then I see a light. It slowly starts to brighten, and I'm back in my room sitting in my computer chair.

Looking around my room, it's just as I left it. Yeval isn't here though.

I feel safe now that I'm back home so I go into the bathroom and splash my face with cool water trying to absorb what just happened.

As I'm walking into the bathroom, it hits me that what I just saw is the kind shit that happens in real fucking life. It ain't like the fucking movies. It's painful, intense, and merciless. I get the feeling that I need to heave so I run over to the toilet.

As I lean over, emptying my stomach of the lunch I had with Ryan, I fear that this isn't the last time I'll be in the Dark Room.

Is Slayer real?

CHAPTER 4

# Father

I'm looking forward to seeing Dr. Jenkins on Monday to discuss what Yeval showed me Thursday evening. I didn't sleep at all that night. I tried going to the casino for a distraction, but I lost nine-hundred dollars and got even more depressed. Then I went home and smoked some pot, hoping it would help me sleep but all it did was make me dwell on it even more.

Today is Saturday. Luckily, I was able to get sleep last night. I purposely slept for twelve hours so I will have the patience to eat lunch with my asshole father.

Morgan didn't come home until this morning. God knows where she was and what she was doing. We had make-up sex, which helped me get into an even better mood than I already was for finally getting enough sleep. She probably only fucked me because I got some more pot.

I'm sitting inside the Hermit Lounge Café with Ryan and my father, Kenneth. Syrup drips from Ryan's lips as he eats his hot-cakes. Asshole (my dad) eats a French-dip, which is what he always eats. I pick at my pepperoni-salami sub, planning on taking it home later because I don't really have an appetite at the moment. I have a hard time eating in front of people I don't like. I'll just pick at my food, waiting for the moment to pass so I can go hang out with people I actually do like.

I haven't talked to Asshole and he hasn't spoken to me. We are both just taking turns talking to Ryan, which is overwhelming the poor kid.

I've been asking Ryan how he liked the movie, what his plans are for the week, and how he likes my new car. Asshole has been talking to him about stupider stuff. Right now, Asshole is asking Ryan about his girlfriend Patty. Like it's any of that asshole's business!

"How long has it been since you two started dating?" Asshole asks.

"We've been boyfriend and girlfriend for almost three years," he says, with food in his mouth. I'm quite impressed, although my relationship with Caroline lasted five years. I want to tell Ryan how impressed I am, but I decide not to because I don't want Asshole to know how I feel.

23

All Asshole says is, "That's good."

There is a short pause, and I realize that Asshole hasn't even attempted to ask about my girlfriend.

"Maybe Morgan and I can take you guys out to the movie," I suggest, trying to impress my father with how good a brother I am. "I'm sure Patty would like that."

"Uh, that's okay, Randy," Ryan says, trying not to crack a smile. "Patty doesn't really like Morgan."

Asshole laughs. I personally think this is unacceptable, even if he does think it's funny. He's encouraging Ryan to be rude.

"I don't really like her much either," Ryan confesses.

Ryan usually isn't rude. I guess he just feels justified in acting like this because my father agrees with him. I would be mad at Ryan but I agree with him too. I don't really like Morgan either. I can just imagine how stupid I must look right now, blank-faced and speechless because of a retard.

"No reason to be sorry, son," Asshole says to Ryan. "I don't think your brother likes her either. Does anybody?"

Instead of socking my dad in his lip, I decide to try and impress him by responding calmly.

"It's hard for me to get offended by Ryan's opinion because he knows Morgan. So does Patty," I say.

Asshole just sits there waiting for me to continue, which is smart, because if he interrupts me (like he usually does), I swear to God I'm going to knock him out of his chair.

"You, on the other hand, don't know her. You're just agreeing with the person who disagrees with me." I put my elbows on the table, which Asshole think is impolite, and stare at him. "Typical," I add.

"You're right," he says. "Maybe I would have a better opinion if you'd act like a son and a boyfriend, and let me get to know your girlfriend for myself."

"Well, maybe if you'd act like a father, I wouldn't be so self-conscious about bringing her around and inviting you over. You're just so quick to judge, it's as if you *want* to dislike me."

Asshole begins shaking his head. "You go out of your way to be a rebel," he says. "It's as if you want to disappoint me."

"Disappoint?" I say. "Oh. I said, 'dislike'. I didn't know I disappoint you too."

"Dad," Ryan interrupts. I'm thankful for the interruption because this was about to get ugly. "You shouldn't say stuff like that." Yes! Ryan is taking my side. "It's good we are here together. Let's not screw it up. I like having both of you around at the same time."

I'm about to calm down when I hear the sound of a triangle. I look around the café to find its source. There's a red figure peeking at me from the corner nearest the bathrooms. It's Yeval.

I excuse myself from the table while Asshole is in the middle of saying something. I walk into the men's bathroom to find Yeval. The Pearl floats in midair by the sink. There is no one else in the bathroom.

"What do you want, Yeval?"

"I have something to show you in the Dark Room," he says in his creepy scratchy voice.

"I'm not going back there after what I saw. Now leave me alone, I'm eating lunch with my brother and father."

"You have to see this. I have something very important to show you."

"I'm never going in the Dark Room again, Yeval."

"Oh yes you will," he says in a threatening tone. "I know it!"

"No I won't," I say, turning around and leaving.

Luckily, Yeval doesn't follow me. I sit back down and wait for Ryan and my dad to finish their lunches, as I box up mine. Neither of them ask why I barely ate my sandwich.

My father and I end up taking Ryan back to Maple Way together since neither of us could agree on who'd take him home. I figure I should take him home because my father picked him up, but Asshole still insisted on doing it. Ryan told us he wanted to walk. So, we all agreed that the three of us would walk to Maple Way together. It's an enjoyable twenty minutes if you're in the right mood.

Asshole and I both say our goodbye to Ryan, and confirm our plans to see him again later in the week separately.

On the walk back few words are exchanged. I comment on how I enjoy walking places. He comments on how nice the day is. I thank him for taking me out to lunch. He tells me it was his pleasure and to take it easy. That's about all I can recall. I notice how neither of us say we enjoyed seeing each other again, or how we should do this again. It kind of makes me sad.

From time to time, I wonder if the hatred between me and my father is mutual. I occasionally question how much my father really hates me, or if even he does. I sometimes think I might not even hate my father at all.

CHAPTER 5

# Newspaper

Last night Yeval tried to talk me into going back to the Dark Room, but I refused again. I ended up taking Morgan to Silver's Casino, where I won two-hundred dollars in blackjack. Morgan was very impressed, telling me how good I am. Stupid cunt. She still has no idea about the nine-hundred dollars I dropped on Thursday night.

We ended up getting toasted at the bar, then returning home to get it on. Because I earned some money, I guess Morgan thought it was a celebration, giving me more than usual. Last night, or early this morning since I suppose it was at about 3:30 am, I rammed Morgan in her tight ass. She lubed my cock up with her mouth, and I lubed her tight ass up with my tongue, fingering it while I kissed her butt-cheeks. I love tossing salad when it's clean, of course.

I get up at 10:30, while Morgan's still asleep, to get the Sunday paper. I make it a goal to read the newspaper everyday so I can: a) stay updated on the events that are happening in the world, and b) feel sophisticated.

It takes me from the front door, where the newspaper is at, to the kitchen counter, where I set the newspaper down, to finally notice the headline on the front page. "SEATTLE SLAYER STRIKES AFTER ALMOST TWENTY YEARS OF SILENCE".

The article reads:
BY SAM FOLEY
*Seattle Times North side bureau*

The city of Seattle thought it was at terms with the notorious Seattle Slayer until Thursday evening when a Kirkland family of three was found murdered in their home. The serial killer's calling card, his name written in his victim's blood, reopened the cold-case.

Chris Sizemore, 32, was discovered beaten to death with a baseball bat found at the scene of the crime. His wife Lynn, 31, and their son Andrew, 4, were also found dead.

The family was not found until Saturday morning, when a neighbor called police after not having seen the couple in a few days. Police arrived at the scene to find the tragic truth of the Sizemore family and the rebirth of the Seattle Slayer.

The last murder by the Seattle Slayer was in early 1990 when two teenage siblings were found murdered in their home. Jim King, 17, was found tied to a chair and shot numerous times in the face. His sister Haley, 16, was found tied in a chair next to her brother with her throat slit. The Seattle Slayer's calling card appeared in their blood on a wall in their living room.

The Seattle Slayer's calling card, which police believe he uses in order to make sure he gets credit for the crimes, has been dated to murders as early as 1975 when the Nolan family of six was found mutilated, their bodies stuffed in their refrigerator, while their limps were found in the freezer. All six of their heads are still missing to this day.

Seattle Slayer is also known to use weapons found at the crime scene. Authorities have confirmed that the baseball bat used in the killings was indeed Sizemore's. Friends of the family say the couple kept a baseball bat by their bed for protection against an intruder. The Sizemore family had filed two robbery reports earlier in the year, but police don't think the incidences are connected.

Detective George Curtis has been working on the Seattle Slayer case since 1979. "I have a lot of confidence in DNA testing and the forensic science we have available. Science has come a long way since the last Slayer incident in 1990. Hopefully, we'll be able to crack the case and put the Seattle Slayer behind bars."

Anxiety suddenly overwhelms me and my stomach begins to pulse, so I run to the toilet. As I lean over the toilet barfing, I ask myself how likely it is that what I read in the article and what I saw in the Dark Room are connected. After a couple of minutes of on and off heaving, I start feeling better.

I find Yeval standing in the doorway when I look up from the toilet.

"They *are* connected," he says with a smile.

"It could be a coincidence."

"You don't believe me?"

"I don't want to believe you."

"I wanted you to come into the Dark Room yesterday in the bathroom," he says. "Remember? At Hermit Lounge."

"Yeah, I remember."

"I had something to show you in the Dark Room."

"What did you have to show me?" I ask, half concerned. All I want is silence to think about what the hell is going on, but fucking Yeval keeps nagging at me. I can't tell Yeval to just go away because then he'll just stay longer.

I hear the sound of a triangle. The Pearl appears in the middle of the bathroom.

"Grab the Pearl and join me in the Dark Room," Yeval says.

"No. I'm not going back to that place."

"But then you won't be able to see the murders."

"Yeah. I don't want to see the murders."

"But I can't show them to just anyone. I have to show them to you."

I stand up and walk over to the sink to brush my teeth and get the puke taste out of my mouth.

"I guess you and Slayer are going to have to enjoy the murders yourselves, because I don't want to watch," I tell him.

"But you can see what's happening," he says to me. "You can prevent the rest."

"Huh?" I ask.

"An elderly man was dropped from the third floor of his four story mansion," he says. "Somebody will find him. Watch for it on the news."

Yeval and the Pearl both vanish into thin air.

"Wait," I yell. "Come back. What do you mean?"

"Who are you talking to?" Morgan asks me, walking into the bathroom.

Sure enough, the news that afternoon reports a man named Edwin Meyer, 87, found on the bottom floor of his mansion. He's found by one of his maids who tells police that he was fine when she left Saturday morning. "SLAYER," is found written on the wood floor in the man's blood. The impact from the fall killed him. Authorities believe that he was thrown from the indoor balcony of the third floor, where his bedroom was located.

Is Yeval telling the truth?

CHAPTER 6

# Appointment

It was a long weekend. Then again, every day is a weekend for a drug-dealer.

I was desperate to speak with Dr. Jenkins over the last few days, but I couldn't get a hold of him. Instead being angry though, I spent all day Saturday and Sunday obsessing that something may have happened to Dr. Jenkins too.

When I arrive at the John Fern Building, room 304, I see that his door is open. Relief washes over me as if it was very unlikely he'd be okay.

Life would be so much better if I didn't worry so much.

That hot bitch receptionist is in the waiting room again. She is putting files away in the filing cabinet. Since she is finally standing, I can get a good look at her ass. Yup. Nice, round, fat and juicy. Just how I like it.

She sees me walk in and smiles at me. This time she is wearing glasses. I'd like to give her a cumshot with those glasses on. That would be hot.

I walk right past her into room 304B, completely ignoring the bitch. This again, satisfies me for some reason.

I enter the room to see Dr. Jenkins looking out the window. I let him enjoy whatever he's looking at, whether that be the birds, a hot bitch in the parking lot, or the Space Needle a few blocks away. I look at my watch. On time as usual.

I quietly take a seat on the leather couch, not making a sound.

"Randy!" Dr. Jenkins says, surprised. "You startled me. You're very quiet."

"Sorry," I say, smiling. "How was your weekend?"

"Fine, fine," he says. We shake hands. "How was yours?"

"Stressful," I say, adjusting myself on the couch.

He sits at Dr. Baker's old desk, now covered with his things. They must have hauled Dr. Baker's stuff out during the weekend and moved his stuff in. Sadness fills me as I look at his computer and his phone on *her* desk; he's here to stay.

I sigh.

"So, what happened?" he asks, opening my file.

I explain to him every detail of what happened. Every single detail. In fact, I repeated a few things just to make sure he hears me right. He stares at me. Is he in disgust? Shock? Both?

"You're joking. You read this in the paper, didn't you." he says, in disbelief.

"Nope," I confirm. "Yeval showed it to me on the day it happened."

"It's just a coincidence."

"It is!" I say hopefully.

"There's no logical reason," he reassures me.

His words comfort me, even though they shouldn't. If he's right, then I'm far crazier than I thought I was. If he's wrong, then the situation is bound to get worse.

"So, what should I do the next time Yeval shows me the Pearl?"

"Did you like what Yeval showed you before?"

"Hell no!" I say, offended that he'd ask such a thing.

"Then ignore Yeval, like you did yesterday." He moves on, as if the problem is solved. "What else did you do this weekend?"

"But Dr. Jenkins, Yeval described to me what Slayer's next move was when I didn't go into the Dark Room."

"Randy, Yeval has brought you nothing but trouble for more than half your life. You need to try and ignore him, because analyzing your thoughts every second of the day is making you miserable, which makes Yeval stronger. Whatever grain of truth is in these images, it's only misleading you."

He's got a point. Even if I'm not crazy and Dr. Jenkins is wrong, I still have no way of proving any of this. But I can't get it out of my mind.

"Have you talked to your father?"

"Yes. We actually had lunch together with Ryan on Saturday."

"How did it go?"

"I have to admit, it was nice seeing him again."

"Do you think he enjoyed seeing you again?"

"Nah. Nothing has changed between us. It's the same old shit."

"Why? Has nothing else changed in your life to satisfy him?" he asks.

"Yeah, I guess. I'm mean, I'm still selling. Ya know."

"Do you plan on getting a real job sooner or later?"

"Sure," I say. "Once I finish my novel, I'm going to get it published and be rich."

"Oh, I see. You like to write?"

"No. I like to read and tell stories."

"What kind of story is this?"

"It's a fantasy," I say, embarrassed by the cliché.

"What's it about?" he asks, as he scribbles something down in the file.

"It has three main characters," I'm starting to get excited, "One is a prince-warrior who survived a shipwreck and is far away from home. Another is an elf who does great magic. The third character is a thief with a golden heart. Their stories all intertwine."

"Interesting," Dr. Jenkins says. I think he's pretending. He's not even looking at me. I'd continue but I know he's not interested.

Time passes and it gets to the part of the appointment when he asks me when I want to return. I make an appointment for next Monday.

On the drive home, Yeval appears in the passenger seat of my car. He brings the Pearl.

"Dr. Jenkins really thinks this is affecting me," I say to Yeval, trying not to get mad.

"Well, it should affect you," he says. "What you saw was horrible."

"You were laughing!"

"I like that stuff."

"I'm not going back into the Dark Room, Yeval. Even if what you show me is true, I can't prove it."

"Did he tell you that?"

"No. That's just something I realized during my appointment."

"Dr. Jenkins doesn't know anything."

"Are you just saying that because he's helping me get rid of you?" I ask.

"I can leave when you want."

"Okay. I want you to leave."

I start up my engine and drive off. He's still there.

"Under one condition," he says.

"I'm not playing anymore of your games, Yeval."

"Come with me into the Dark Room and I will leave you alone."

The Pearl appears. It floats between Yeval and me.

"You'll never bother me again?" I ask, looking back and forth from the road to him.

"Never again."

I pull over to the side of the road, grab the Pearl and enter the Dark Room.

## CHAPTER 7

# Garage

"So, you'll never bother me again, right?" I make sure, looking down at Yeval, who sits in the red chair of the Dark Room.

"Never again," he says.

Waiting for the lights to dim and the yellow curtain to open, my leg starts to shake nervously. I walk over to and look out the window on my right. The horses (or unicorns) are still galloping in the golden field. It is day now and the yellow summer sun floats slowly west. The woman in orange still watches the horses. I see now, which I didn't notice before, that she is pregnant.

"It's going to start," Yeval shouts worriedly, not wanting me to miss a single frame.

I make my way to the chair slowly, not wanting to watch what I am about to see. Before sitting down, I look out the window to my left. It is still a gloomy sight, with a dirt road leading to nothing but hills. The burnt tree stands alone in the dirt.

"Hurry! Sit." Yeval says.

The room goes dark and the yellow curtain opens.

I take a seat in the other red chair.

On the screen a blue car in a parking garage. I can't make out the make or year because I'm looking at it from the side. I'm looking at it from the driver's side of the vehicle, where I notice that the driver's seat window has been broken.

"Is this Slayer?" I make sure.

"Yes. Stop asking questions and watch," Yeval whispers.

He wants me to be shocked, startled, surprised, sickened, speechless, scared, shitless, and a bunch of other adjectives that start with an s. The reason I care about what Yeval wants is because if I do give him what he wants, he's more likely to keep his word actually leave me alone, whereas if I kept asking questions he might keep asking me to come to the Dark Room. So I decide to play it his way.

I can't see Slayer's reflection in the window, which disappoints me because I want to see what the bastard looks like, and I know he wouldn't be wearing his white face-painted disguise like the last time I saw him because he is in a public parking garage. In fact, I notice he's wearing a wool suit this time.

The parking garage is empty, with the exception of Slayer, the cars, and a man walking to his car. This poor man is going to be the victim.

Slayer speaks for the first time. "Excuse me, sir."

Slayer has a medium pitched voice, that sounds surprisingly comforting. I'd imagine such an evil person to have an ugly, scratchy, low voice—like Yeval. I expect him to look scary and ugly like Yeval too.

"Yes?" the man responds, a kind smile on his face. The man is in his mid-thirties, has curly-blond hair, blue eyes, is about 5'10, and about 175 pounds.

"My name is…" Slayer begins, "Yeval Mann. I work on the fifth floor. I've seen you around."

Slayer holds out his hand.

"Oh. Uh, I'm Jason Ramsey," the man says, shaking Slayer's hand. Jason looks at Slayer suspiciously, noticing that he's wearing gloves. "I haven't seen you here before." Jason pulls his hand away, slightly suspicious. "So, what can I do you for?"

"It appears somebody broke into my car sometime during the day," Slayer says, trying to sound victimized. "May I use your cell-phone to contact the police?"

Slayer turns around and begins walking back to the car. Jason follows.

"Sure you may use my cell phone."

Jason hands Slayer his cell-phone, and Slayer opens it and pretends to dial.

"You said your name was Yeval? Cool name. Never heard it before. Where is it from?"

"Um, British," Slayer responds absently.

Jason sees the broken window. "Oh dude, that sucks."

"Yeah," Slayer says, bending over to pick up a large piece of shattered glass. "You know what else sucks?"

Jason squints his eyes and shrugs his shoulders, asking for the answer in body-language.

"Being blind, bitch!" Slayer screams, trying not to laugh while speaking. Out of his other hand appears a bottle of mace, which he sprays in Jason's eyes.

"What the fuck, man!?" Jason yells angrily, stumbling backwards.

Slayer leaps forward and pierces the victims throat. A low soft crumbling sound can be heard as the glass grinds through Jason's thyroid. Jason takes about five gasping breathes and drops to the ground. Compared to what the Sizemore Family went through, Jason's death is peaceful.

There is no blood. Slayer kneels over Jason's dead body and tries to remove the piece of glass. He becomes frustrated after a couple of minutes because the glass is lodged too deep in Jason's neck to remove with gloved-fingers. Slayer then pushes down on Jason's neck with both of his palms, pushing the glass deeper in his neck.

"Fuck," I hear Slayer mumble.

Slayer tries to finger the wound, which helps draw some blood, but not nearly enough. So Slayer rips the skin from the wound on Jason's neck with his latex-gloved hands. Blood squirts everywhere as he peels the skin from Jason's neck, revealing muscle and arteries. Slayer dips his hand into the bloody mess. On the pavement, Slayer writes his signature.

Taking Jason's phone, Slayer dials 911. The operator answers, "911 emergency." To which Slayer whispers, "Slayer," then hangs up.

The screen goes black and I'm back in my car.

***

I blacked out for quite a while apparently because there are six people surrounding my car worriedly. The sound of an ambulance approaches.

I smile at one person in embarrassment. I can feel myself beginning to blush, so I immediately start my car and speed off.

Yeval is no longer in the passenger's seat.

As I drive, I hope I will never see Yeval again. I hope I'll never be in the Dark Room again. I hope Yeval stuck to his word.

Only time will tell if what I just saw will really happen. But I know it did...

37

CHAPTER 8

# Time

A month since I was in the Dark Room with Yeval and I haven't seen him since. I believe he kept his promise.

Over the last month I have: written six chapters of my book, attended Dr. Baker's funeral, lost $5000 at the casino, sold drugs, took drugs, been to five Dr. Jenkins appointments, smuggled eighteen cannabis plants across the Canada-Washington border, *accidentally* downloaded gay-porn, hung out with Ryan four times, saw Asshole (my father) only once, joined a softball team, got kicked off the softball team for saying "fuck you" to the umpire, went to the library on several occasions, studied the history of the Seattle Slayer, applied for several jobs, bought a journal, fell down the stairs, cried from depression twice, and jogged everyday.

It was around six o'clock when I realized that I hadn't been jogging today. But I don't like jogging between three and seven because of rush-hour. The city of Seattle has one of the worst rush-hours in the country. People, eager to get home after a hard day's work, only become crankier sitting in traffic. I have almost been hit by a car at least one time every time I jog during rush hour. So fuck it.

Right now I'm at the library surfing the net and picking up orders of books, CDs, and DVDs. The CDs I picked up were "Bringing it All Back Home" by Bob Dylan, "Doggy Style" by Snoop Dogg, "Sports" by Huey Lewis & the News, "Piper at the Gates of Dawn" by Pink Floyd, "Havaña Daydreamin'" by Jimmy Buffett, "At Folsom Prison" by Johnny Cash, "Me Against the World" by Tupac Shakur, "Houses of the Holy" by Led Zeppelin, "Ready to Die" by the Notorious B.I.G., "Birth of the Cool" by Miles Davis.

The DVDs I got were two of my personal favorites, both starring Robert De Niro (the greatest actor ever), "Taxi Driver" (the greatest movie ever made, though the copy I got was of extremely poor picture and sound quality), and the "Godfather" *trilogy* though I just wanted the part two, the best of the trilogy, but the library shipped me all three. Another DVD I got was "Dancer in the Dark", another fave of my, starring Björk the critically acclaimed Icelandic singer, and directed by Lars Von Trier whom also directed "Breaking the Waves", another fantastic film, and whom also broke up with his pregnant wife to move in with their much younger babysitter back in 1996. The fourth DVD I received is a documentary on the Seattle Slayer made back in 1993 called "He Awaits: Studying the Seattle Slayer", which I know will be out of date, but the title is just so damn intriguing.

I received two books, both on the Seattle Slayer. The first "The Seattle Slayer Encyclopedia" copyrighted in 2004, examines all *public* information concerning the Seattle Slayer as well as the background of people who were taken in for questioning. The second, "Serial Killers and Their Ways" might be a yawner because it only has one chapter strictly concerning the Seattle Slayer, but the whole book looks at how the killers act, why they act the way they do, how they can be stopped, and what their next move will often be. Both books had unusually long holds on them; they took a couple of weeks to receive.

There was a half-hour news special last night about the return of the Seattle Slayer. It went into how the Seattle Slayer (now and in the past) would go on a spree of killing two to ten victims, then stop for a few months or even years, and then continue another spree. They interviewed psychologists and none of them had one conclusive answer as to why the Slayer does what he does and what he will do next. All of the interviewees' faces were blurred, in fear that they might be the next victim. The Seattle Slayer, according to every source I have read, strikes randomly and uses a weapon from the murder scene to kill his victims. Both are unusual as most serial killers have a ritual for what type of victim they target (mostly women and children) and their methods. This scares the psychologists the most because they know that Slayer is stronger in his will to attack men as well. He is also more willing to take risks as he kills in different ways with different weapons in different settings. The whole topic sends shivers down the spines of everyone, including me.

Upon reading the books I check out from the library, curled up in my bed like a little bookworm faggot, I learned that the Seattle Slayer is left-handed. I am left handed too. So is Dr. Jenkins and my father. So is Ken Griffey Jr. Bill Clinton too.

A lot of serial killers tend to abuse their victims sexually before (or sometimes after) they are murdered. This ritual is done to make the victim feel powerless, as that's how most killers feel about themselves against the world. Slayer, according to the sources I've read, has never left any clue that investigators could tie to sexual-abuse. It is believed that Slayer commits these murders for his own enjoyment. He doesn't need to feel powerful or secure because he naturally feels that he is always in power. The book, "Serial Killers and Their Ways", labels the Seattle Slayer as an unusual serial killer.

A small section in "The Seattle Slayer Encyclopedia", entitled "Social Slayer":

If someone were to have a run-in with the Slayer in a social setting, he would probably appear as an outgoing and confident individual. It is likely that if you befriended the mysterious Seattle Slayer, you would never see any signs nor would you be a target because Slayer knows the odds of getting caught are greater when you murder somebody you know or have been seen with.

A lot of serial killers tend to be loners, drifters and strugglers. With the lack of evidence in such messy crimes scenes, Slayer is probably somebody who works in law (be that in the police department, judicial or military).

It's almost as if the author of the book is impressed by the Seattle Slayer. The question I have, which "Slayer Encyclopedia" disappointedly doesn't discuss, is why he disappeared for two decades? Did he move away? Did he get arrested for something else? Did he retire? Die?

I'm quite burnt out on the Seattle Slayer for one day, so I put the book down, turn off the light, and try to go to sleep.

I can't stop thinking about Slayer, and how cool it would be if I caught him. I would be the coolest person in the world. I would get a medal of honor—maybe from the president? I'd be happy getting it from the governor. It'd have to be the mayor at least. Then again, I guess the thought of stopping somebody from killing others is better than a medal or recognition.

The room is dark. I'm starting to feel depressed, scared, sick, sad, guilty. I begin to wonder how I'm going to die. There is no question, I *will* die and there is no way out of it. How and when are the only questions I can ask. The hope of dying painlessly and fulfilled haunts me to the point that I regret who I am and I start to hate myself again. I almost went a year without hating myself. Hating myself equals suicidal. Being suicidal equals mood-swings and self-destruction.

I stare at the ceiling for forty-five minutes lost in my thoughts of despair. I look at the fake plastic glow-in-the-dark stars Morgan glued up there, and I'm even more depressed because it reminds of when, as a child, Mom lifted me to the ceiling so I could glue the glow-in-the-dark stars she bought me at Fred Meyer's to my bedroom ceiling.

The stars are glowing brighter than usual. It takes me about ten minutes to figure out that the extra brightness isn't coming from the fake stars on my ceiling. It's the Pearl floating in the middle of my room.

Yeval stands at the doorway, staring at me with a big ugly grin on his face. His eyes reflect off the glow.

"Hello, Randy," he says. "The time has come. Touch the Pearl and come with me into the Dark Room."

He broke his promise.

CHAPTER 9

# Café

As I lay in bed, the Pearl hovering over my feet and Yeval smiling snidely at me, I realize I still didn't run today. I don't want to go in the Dark Room ever again and I don't want to see or talk to Yeval ever again. So, I jump out of bed wearing a pair of sweats, a sleeveless shirt I got from a tennis tournament eight years ago and a pair of slippers, and run out of my apartment. Hopefully Yeval won't follow me. Running seems to help with my stress.

After circling my block three times, my toes begin to blister and I can feel the pavement under my feet through holes that are developing in the soles of my slippers. Since three times around my block isn't shit for me, I decide to cut across the street into the Oliver Stone Park so I can run on the grass.

During the day, Oliver Stone Park is gorgeous. The grass is short and dark-green, people always pick up their dogs' shit, the restrooms are well-laundered and the gazebo roofs have no moss on them. At night however, Oliver Stone Park is like the Dark Room. As I jog through, I get a tour of the shit that goes down there after dusk.

On the park bench sit three men and a woman who are passing a syringe. Two of them lay back with their eyes closed, while the woman is using the needle. The fourth person is anxiously waiting his turn to shoot up. He sees me and shouts, "Run Forest, run!"

I sarcastically say, out of breath, "Yeah, let's shoot some heroin, that's cool."

The junky tries to think of a good come back, but all the fucker thinks to say is, "Fuck you."

"Getting HIV is even cooler, cocksucker," then I give him the middle finger. "Enjoy your high, bitch."

My feet feel better so I decide to run through the forested area of the park where I see three twinks having their fun against the masculine tree

I named Lenny. The faggot in the middle has his pants down, and is getting his small cock sucked by another faggot, jacking himself off. Both of their eyes are closed in pleasure. The two remind me of Carson Daly. The third gaylord stands behind the one getting his cock sucked. He has long hair and a beard, and is obviously much older than the other two. He pulls his pants down to reveal his small limp dick, "Yeah, run cutie. Running is good for you." He then blows me a kiss. Queers don't bother me the least bit, so all I say (contemplating whether or not to say it) is, "Get a room and use a condom." I want to tell them that they could get HIV, but I figure they already know that and don't care.

As I near the other end of the forested part of the park, which is also another entrance to the park I see somebody standing in the bushes. Because it's so dark, I'm unable to see his face. I can hear Yeval, but can't see him. "Stop! Look!" Yeval's voice repeatedly says. But I don't stop and look. I just keep running.

I run out of the park, onto Main Street. I'm pretty tired, but since Yeval is still talking to me, I'm still stressed and frustrated. I can see Hermit Lounge Café a few blocks away so I decide to stop for a drink.

I enter the Café sweaty and out of breath. It is obvious I've been jogging. There are like five holes on the souls of my slippers. The bar is pretty crowded, even for a Saturday night. I take a seat at one of my booths, extremely thirsty, and order a Corona.

Sitting alone in the bar, eavesdropping on the conversations to the left, right and behind me, I notice that all these people are talking about the Seattle Slayer. It makes me feel like less of a psycho because I'm not the only one fascinated by him. But it also upsets me that we all (yes, including me) are more focused on the notoriety of the killer than those who have been killed, or the fact that any one of us Seattleites could be his next victim.

Over the course of the next few hours, conversations break off into new ones, and I am now talking it up with four gentlemen all older than myself. We discuss Slayer, along with other political issues like marijuana legalization, the president, why nudity is taboo, and why violence sells.

It is now 10:30, and one of the waiters announces on the microphone at the small stage, located at the East side of the bar (near where Ryan, Asshole and I sat) that it's time to play Dupez La Foule (French for "Trick The Crowd"...or is it "Deceive The Crowd"?). Whoever could stump the crowd with a question would win fifty dollars plus a drink.

People would go up there and say stuff mostly about movies or music like "Name the killer on 'Nightmare on Elm Street'" which is so obviously Freddy Kruger. Another question, a really good one, was to name all four songs from the Beatles' White Album that had female names in the title. I got "Dear Prudence" and "Julia" but I forgot about "Sexy Sadie" and "Martha My Dear". Luckily, a few other people in the crowd knew the answer. I decided to go on stage, a little drunk, and make an attempt to stump the crowd. I decided to ask a music question as well, "Name the first person to do 'R-E-S-P-E-C-T'?" The crowd shouted Aretha Franklin. I responded, happily, that that was the wrong answer. I pointed out that Otis Redding wrote and recorded the first version of "Respect" (which appeared on "Otis Blue" in 1966). A bartender and a cook confirmed the answer and that was that. People were quite impressed. I walked off stage feeling smarter than everybody, and one of the waiters handed me a fifty dollar bill. Sweet.

The guys I am sitting with bought me some drinks, and we all got faded. I am on my seventh Corona and third Heineken when my moment of fame ended. Everybody's the attention is on somebody who announced that the Seattle Slayer had struck again. Everybody goes silent for five seconds, and then they start talking again. "Turn on the news!" a drunk says to the bartender.

Channel 7 interrupted whatever show was airing to report the breaking news. At this point, details are limited. Coverage simply aired firemen putting out a fire in a upper-suburban home, with the caption on the screen, "Crime-scene of the new Slayer murder". I turn from my front row seat in the booth to see almost the entire café crowded behind me, staring intently at the television. I understand the shock, but these people are watching it like it's entertainment. It's as if we are the crowd watching the Seattle Slayer battle the investigators. Thankfully, no investigators agree to an interview with a beautiful bitch news-reporter, so Channel 7 quickly returns to the regular show and the crowd breaks up.

I sit at the bar, not wanting to talk to anybody, feeling even worse than I did before. Should I have grabbed the Pearl? Did Yeval really have something of importance to show me? Was that man in the park possibly the Seattle Slayer? Maybe it is my fault my mother is dead. Is Ryan retarded because of me? Is this why my father hates me? Did Caroline break up with me because she thought I wasn't happy, or was she the one who *really*

45

wasn't happy? Does the casino still have me down over $300? Would I take pleasure in watching a porno where a woman plays being raped? Am I a bad person? Do I really mean well, or do I just think I do? Why do I throw up so much? How will I die? I wonder what would happen if I just walked up to the bartender and spit in his face? Would I cry in pain if Morgan chopped off my penis? Is my penis an attractive size? Do I love Morgan?

"Randy," I hear a voice say.

There are millions of Randy's in this world, so I just ignore it.

Have I already had the best sex of my life? Would I have sex with a fourteen year old if she was extremely hot? Will I ever see anything funnier than that time I saw a 330 pound fat kid (with a beat red scared face, nonetheless) trying to run from a pitbull, who ended up tackling him to the ground and tearing apart his pants because the dog smelt hamburgers that the fat kid stuffed in his pants (if I were the fat kid I would've thrown the patties at the dog)?

"Randy. It is you! Randy Mulray!" say this beautiful voice.

I turn around to see who it is. My heart skips a beat and my stomach flexes unconsciously. It is Caroline Wooden, my ex-girlfriend and long lost love.

"Caroline, hello," I say. I'm in a mixture of happiness and grief. I dream about seeing her everyday, but I don't want her to see me like this, depressed and sweaty.

"Is anyone sitting here?" she asks, already taking a seat.

"No! Please sit," I say, trying to pull her chair out like a gentleman. I realize I can't do this sitting down, so I stand up to gather enough strength to push her chair in. I hope I don't look like an ass. I hope she knows how tough I am.

I try to think of what to say before I sit down, but instead just sit. We sit in silence for a moment. Is it a good silence? She looks very happy to see me. Does she know I'm a drug-dealer? I play off the silence as if I'm admiring her dirty blonde hair, her sparkling blue eyes, and her pearly white teeth (which I really am), then I turn to the bartender and say, "Two Red Hooks, please." I turn back to Caroline and smile, realizing I didn't ask if she wanted a drink. I save myself by saying, "Red Hook is still your favorite, right?" She nods, yes. I'm so cool. The reason I ordered Red Hooks was because it used to be Caroline's favorite.

"I remember Red Hook is your favorite...or *was*," I say coyly.

"Very good! What else do you remember," she say, genuinely impressed...I think.

"I remember good times," I say I'm trying to be suave but end up being a corny fucking dork. "What are you up to these days?"

"Well, I work at the bank. I have a wonderful daughter named Jane. She's three now."

I do a great job of hiding how upset I am. I wanted to be the father of her child. She is the only person I've ever wanted to be the mother of my child. But it's too late and there's nothing I can do. I think when I get home I might kill myself.

"You have a family?" I ask.

"No. Divorced," she says. Thank God for that, but then again, *I* was the one who should've married her. Why didn't she choose me? Am I better than her ex-husband? Should I hang myself? Slit my wrists? Overdose on my anti-depressants?

"I'm sorry. We both know breakups are hard."

"Well, it wasn't that hard losing him," she thankfully says. I wonder what she means but I don't linger on the thought too long.

The bartender delivers our drinks. I realize that this is my eleventh beer and wonder if Caroline can tell. We both thank the bartender, and she continues.

"I've had harder breakups." I smile at her, admiring how beautiful she is. Morgan is hot, but Caroline is gorgeous. Morgan is like a porn star, while Caroline is like an angel. Morgan offers fantasy fulfillment sex, while Caroline offers beauty, compassion, wisdom, talent, humor and comfort. She's still a shorty, a little over five feet and weighing about 125 pounds. She is tiny, petite, with the perfect amount of imagery on her. Her tits aren't as big as Morgan's, but I take comfort in the fact that Caroline's B-cups will still be perky by the time she's fifty, while Morgan's DD-cups will be sagging to her knee-caps.

"You single?" I ask, not realizing I said it out loud.

"Dates here and there. Nobody special," she says. "You?"

"I'm with somebody," I respond. It feels like a confession.

"Good for you."

I want this conversation to go on for some reason, so I say shamefully, "No. It's just an excuse not to be alone. It's not cruel though. She's using me too."

"Oh," she says. I hope she doesn't think I'm a jerk for what I just said.

"It's good to hear things are going well for you."

I take a sip of my beer and almost spit it out because it tastes like sour feet. Caroline laughs.

"Gross," I say, wiping my mouth with my shirt (I wonder if she finds that unattractive), "Does yours suck too?"

"Yeah," she says, still laughing at me. "Just trying not to be rude to you or the house. But since you agree, yeah, it's pretty bad."

We both laugh. It's kind of a romantic moment.

"So, what are you doing these days, Randy?"

"Uh, I am, uh, a, uh, I spend my time writing," I say, hoping she still can't tell when I lie.

"What do you write?" she asks, intrigued.

"I enjoy writing fiction."

"Yeah. What kind of fiction?"

I decide not to pitch my story because I'm already worn thin after pitching it to Dr. Jenkins, Morgan, and Ryan. Instead, I take another route. "Anything really. I take a lot of my ideas from things that have happened to me. Sometimes it can be funny, like a comedy. Sometimes it can be heartbreaking, like a drama."

"When have you suffered a broken heart, Randy?" she asks, I think seriously.

"You," I whip back. The conversation had now gone from casual to serious.

"Me? But you had me and it didn't work out."

"I didn't listen. 'You don't know what you've got until it's gone.' It breaks my heart to know that I let something come between us. It breaks my heart that the last five years we've been separated could've been us building a family if we had stayed together.

"I did some bad things. Sold drugs. Did a few weeks in prison. You stuck with me through thick and thin. You stayed faithful and honest, when you deserved someone so much better. You'll always be in my heart," I finally stop, wondering if she feels how I feel.

"That's the nicest thing I've heard in years," she says. She knows me well and she knows I'm telling the truth.

"You've heard better," I say jokingly, trying not to be too Kumbaya.

She looks me in the eye and says, "The last time was when we were together."

We make plans to see each other again. I stumble and skip my drunk ass home feeling happier than I've ever been. When I get to my apartment I realize that I locked myself out because I didn't take my keys when Yeval appeared in my bedroom. Morgan still isn't home either.

I curl up on my Family Guy doormat like a dog and pass out.

CHAPTER 10

# Casino

The security at Long John Silver's Casino had to think a while about letting me in after the outburst I had with another customer the last time I was there. I was in the Texas Hold'em tournament when a guy insulted me for calling his all in. There was an ace and two nines out on the table, and the douche-bag goes all in. I hold A-10 off suit, but I don't think the douche-bag has the nine, so I call. He shows me pocket-kings. The dealer shows the turn and the river, and I end up winning the pot with a pair of aces. Lucky for the douche-bag, he had more chips than me so he was still in the game. But he says to me, "You called an all-in with that! That's not even a good kicker." Appalled by his moronic comment, I reply, "Yeah, let's go all in with kings when there is a possibility that your opponent is holding two aces or three nine. Your odds weren't so good. You shouldn't have gone all in." He doesn't say anything, probably because he *knows* I am right.

Anyway, the douche-bag and I make it to the last table. It's down to about nine players. I'm short-stacked because of a few suck-outs but don't hold it against anybody. So anyway, I go all in with pocket queens, and the douche-bag calls me with A-10! He is drawing dead until the river, where he hits his ace. The dealer, a very sexy oriental bitch, looks at me in sorrow as if it was her fault for putting that ace out there. So, I say to the douche-bag, patronizing the faggot for what he said to me earlier, "You played that. That's not even a good kicker." Feeling disrespected or something, he responds, "Don't be a smartass." So I tell him how I'm going to beat the living shit out of him and choke him to death by shoving his chips down his throat. He stands up defensively and I laugh at him. By this time, security quietly and gently escorts me out of the casino. I was very peaceful with the two security guards, even though I could have whooped both of their asses.

Today is the Sunday before Labor Day, and the tournament players are lined up out the door. Some of them will be alternates. Others won't get in at all. Lucky for me, I came an hour early because I knew it was going to be packed. It's a $50 buy-in, and if the rumor is true there are 180 playing, meaning first place gets almost $3600!

I sit at a table with eleven people. There is one heavy-set guy in his early thirties, a loud Vietnamese guy sitting to the right of me, and the rest are old men. The dealer is a young Peruvian guy named Angel.

It's only ten minutes into the tournament, and I haven't played a single hand yet. I am in the small blind and am dealt pocket queens. An old guy raises, and I, because of my bad luck with QQ last time, just call. On the flop comes a queen of spades, a ten of clubs, and a five of spades. Three Queens! I decide to be a nice guy and just check my set of queens. The old guy goes all in and I gladly call him. I reveal my queens, and the old guys rolls his eyes almost mucking his hand, but ends up showing me pocket eights. The Vietnamese guy's slanted eyes widen when he sees my queens, and he whispers, "Ooh!" The turn comes a two of spades. The old guy says, "Come on spades!" I realize now that he's on a runner-runner flush draw. The river comes a king of spades, and the old faggot wins the pot. The Vietnamese guy next to me pats the table where my cards are, indicating that I played my hand well and that it's wasn't my fault I lost. But that lazy compliment does nothing for my rage. "You went all-in on pocket eights with two over-cards, after I checked! You suck," I say bitterly to the old faggot. The old faggot responds, stacking his chips, "I was trying to bluff and I got lucky. Sorry." I stand up, absorbing what just happened and scream, "You are a shitty poker player!"

I smile at Angel who glances back and forth from me to security, and I rip my cards in half. He swallows, anxiously waiting for security. I kick the shit out of my chair, breaking all four legs and head for the exit, my face beat red in anger. I see a sexy trophy wife checking me out from the tables (I think she's an alternate), staring at my ass. So, I decide to walk up to her, eating her eggs and hash browns with her rich muscular husband, and scream in her face, "What are you looking at!"

A security guard approaches me, telling me to get out. I stand there, trying to think of what to say but before I think of anything, he grabs me by the elbow and drags me to the exit. Because I'm so tough, the security guard expends a lot of effort to drag me. Meanwhile, I'm thinking of how I can get revenge for such a bad suck-out.

"Don't come back. You hear?" says the security guard, as he's pushing me out the door.

After spending a half hour pouring the casino's outside garbage all over the parking lot, I finally get the idea to go back in and scatter everybody's chips together and ruin the tournament. So, I stand by the door waiting for somebody to leave. Finally someone opens the door and exits, and I sprint in before it closes. I speed past the same security guard who immediately notices me, saying, "Goddamnit! Call the police." I run up to the table I was at, and I jump on the table, throwing my arms and legs at every chip in reach, scattering them everywhere.

Some asshole, maybe the Vietnamese guy, punches me in my ribs and I go down laughing. Three security guards grab me from the table, and I fart loudly while they carry me. They take me into a hallway where I presume they're going to wait with me until the police arrive. I whine, "I have to go pee!" But they tell me to fuck myself. I get the idea that peeing on them might help me escape. So I unzip my fly, and pull out my great big penis and start pissing everywhere. Like I assumed, the security guards jump away in disgust. One of them actually screams like a little girl.

I put my slong away, and book for the exit. As I run through the casino again I make sure to knock over some more stacks. One of the poker players tries to catch me, but I dodge him and exit the casino.

As I walk home satisfied, I wonder if Slayer gets that kind of thrill when he kills somebody. I know what I did pissed people off but it please me. I wonder if murder pleases Slayer. What would the world be like if we all just did what we pleased?

I finally get home. There is a moment of sheer panic when I think that I might have forgotten my keys inside again or maybe lost them at the casino. But I didn't. They're right here in my pocket. Relief washes over me as I unlock my apartment and walk in only to be welcomed by Yeval and the Pearl...

CHAPTER II

# Exit

A prostitute who introduces herself as Tracy gets in the passenger's seat of Slayer's car. Because I am watching through Slayer's eyes, I can't tell what kind of car he is driving. It is definitely a luxury vehicle because of the leather interior, electric speedometer and tachometer, and a gadget that tells you how many miles your car has left until it is empty (something my 2007 Chrysler Sebring doesn't even have), but I can't tell the make or model.

Tracy is fuckable. She's in her early forties, dirty blonde hair with bleach-blonde highlights, tanned, gray-eyes and weighing about 150 pounds. I don't think *I'd* ever fuck her, but a woman with her looks can make a decent living giving head to guys who are pathetic enough to pay for it. I think fucking a pocket-pussy is less degrading than *paying* for the real thing. I mean, who knows what STDs this bitch is crawling with. Goneria? HIV? Herpes? Hepatitis C? I'd rather fuck a toy, than have to pay someone to have sex with me. That's pathetic. Then again, if the whore was hot enough, I'd probably fuck her.

Sitting in the Dark Room, I stare at Tracy with rage. How bad could life have been for her to sink to this level? There is a thought that dangles in the back of my mind telling me that perhaps this is for the best, perhaps Tracy is better off dead. The thought comforts me and I actually think it to be true for a moment but I realize the truth. Poor Tracy is going to die a painful death, while I sit here and watch. She won't ever get the chance to put her life back together. Her life must have been really bad but it just got a whole lot worse.

The two enter a hotel room right off of I-5 called Jones Inn. As Slayer holds Room 8 open for Tracy, I notice a large suit case in his left hand. I don't bother wondering what it could be because I know I'll eventually find out.

As Tracy strips to nothing by the bed, Slayer is sitting at the table pouring two glasses of champagne. Three pills dissolve in the glass that Slayer is now handing to Tracy. Tracy guzzles it down.

"Lay down," Slayer says, sipping his champagne slowly. She lays down on the bed with her bra and underwear still on. She pulls off her underwear slowly, revealing her hairy but surprisingly clean vagina.

"Come on," she says, opening her thighs. "Give it to me."

Slayer walks back over to the table and sits down.

"Touch yourself," he says, adjusting himself in the chair.

Tracy closes her eyes and begins rubbing her vagina with her right hand. As she moans, she replaces her right hand with her left. She brings her right hand to her mouth and starts licking the cunt from her fingers. This arouses me slightly.

She does this for a couple of minutes before she slows down and passes out, legs still open. Slayer walks up to her unconscious body and pours a few drops of champagne on her forehead. She doesn't move. Slayer pinches her shoulder hard. Tracy still doesn't move. She is out cold.

Slayer ties Tracy's wrists and ankles to each of the four bedposts with plastic zip-ties. He sets his suitcase on the table and opens it up. In the suitcase are a pack of AAA batteries, a hammer, a screwdriver, a chrome .45, a kitchen knife, a saw, rope, a camera, duct tape, a blow torch, and much more. Slayer removes a needle and thread from the suitcase.

For the next ten minutes, he carefully sews Tracy's mouth and eyes shut. I already know what sound to expect when Tracy tries to scream through her stitched lips.

Still unconscious, Slayer carefully cuts open Tracy's abdomen, slicing from her groin to sternum, careful not to disturb any intestines. He gently wipes blood off that begins to pour from her stomach's opening. He lays down next to her on the bed, and strokes her shiny blonde hair. It reminds me of Caroline's.

Tracey finally awakes, wiggling her head violently trying to see. Her muffled screams are just as painful and helpless as I imagined. Tears drip through the stitches in her eyes. Slayer nibbles on her ear affectionately and whispers, "It's okay, sweetie. You're going to be okay. Just calm down. Can you calm down for me, sweetie? I won't hurt you anymore."

Tracy's panicking begins to ease, finding Slayer's words comforting. Stupid whore. You're going to die! Use the muscles in your jaw to rip through your sewn lips and scream your lungs out! Stupid whore!

"Do you want to see?" Slayer says.

Tracey nods her head up and down urgently.

"Now this is going to hurt a little, but it will be okay," Slayer warns. "Are you ready, sweetie? I'll try to make it as painless as possible."

Tracey nods.

Still lying on the bed next to her, Slayer removes a scalpel from his back pocket and begins unstitching Tracey's right eye. She lays still, but moans in agony.

Her eye is open.

"Can you see?" Slayer asks.

She nods her head, staring at him in fear.

"Okay," he begins, "Let me slide you up." Slayer lifts her back and moves the pillow behind her up so she is sitting her. Tracey can now see that her stomach has been cut open. She begins screaming through her closed mouth again. Blood begins to drip out of the stitch wounds from her mouth as she screams.

Slayer walks over to his suitcase while Tracey is staring at her own intestines in shock. Slayer removes a sparkling silver hatchet. He strikes down on her left foot. Her ring and pinky toe fall off, and blood sprays everywhere. The spraying from the wound soon softens into a fountain, pumping out blood in synch with her racing pulse.

Slayer throws the bloodied hatchet back in the suitcase. He then removes a garden hose from the bottom of the suitcase and unwinds it. He walks into the bathroom and hooks one end of the hose up to the facet. He takes the other end of the hose and crams it up Tracey's vagina. He turns the hose on.

It isn't long after that there is a pop sound, and light-red bloodied-water starts to pour out of the opening of her stomach. Bloodied-water also leaks from her vagina. I'm assuming that the cervix worked as a wall and just gave in when the water pressure was too much.

Tracey is still breathing. Her open eye flickers as though she's having a seizure. I think I can see a thumping in her stomach.

Slayer turns the facet off.

He lays on the wet blood-soak bed with Tracey, and he giggles as he's fingering her intestines.

I close my eyes. It has gotten to the point where I can't watch anymore.

"Watch!" Yeval yells at me.

I simply can't. Knowing that this is really happening, for the life of me I can't watch this shit anymore. I get up from the red chair and walk back and forth in a panic. How will I ever get this out of my head.

"Sit down!" Yeval demands.

As I walk back and forth, ignoring Yeval, I see a sparkle from beneath my chair.

"Just sit down," Yeval yells, knowing that I noticed something.

I get down on my hands and knees and take a closer look. It is a ruby tucked next to the front left leg of the red chair. I'm about to touch it when Yeval yells, "No! Don't touch it!"

"Why?" I ask, now curious.

"Just don't!"

I stare at Yeval. His eyes are red with anger. What is this ruby and why is Yeval so defensive of it? Why didn't I notice it before? After a few long seconds, I decide to ignore Yeval and grab the ruby. As I grab it, Yeval yells, "No!"

I stare at this beautiful ruby in my hand. It's the same size as the Pearl, except it is cut in the shape of a diamond and is much lighter. I look up from my hand I notice I am back in my apartment. The ruby has disappeared.

I have now found an exit from the Dark Room.

CHAPTER 12

# Located

I grab my keys, book out the front door, hop in my car and drive to Jones Inn. I park across the street and wait for something to happen. Staring at room number eight, I prepare myself to finally see what Slayer looks like. If I do see him, I expect him to be ugly and scary.

I have been here for forty-seven minutes when the clock hits midnight. I fall asleep at about twelve-forty, and wake at seven-twenty. I'm about to drive off when I notice a maid approaching room eight.

She knocks on the door and nobody answers. I suppose that she assumes the guests are still sleeping, so she goes to the next room to deliver towels and sheets. Twenty minutes later she comes back, and knocks on the door four times. She unlocks the door and enters the room. Even from across the street in my car, I can hear the maid scream.

The maid comes running out of the motel room in tears, covering her mouth. The look on her face is actually kind of funny. When people are genuinely frightened, they get a moronic look on their faces that is quite humorous. Their eyes widen and then squint, and you can see them quietly gasping for air. And when it's panic, it's either extremely serious or extremely funny. In this particular case, it's funny because the maid is in such deep shock, she doesn't even have the thought-process at the moment to notify anyone. She just makes circles around her towel cart until she finally gathers enough of her wits to sprint to the main office.

Police, fire trucks, and an ambulance are at the scene in less than a minute. Detectives arrive also. The law enforcement are all professional. I admit if it were me, I'd be panicking like that maid. None of the medics, police, detectives or firefighters vomit or scream. I saw about three or four of them walk out of the motel room shaking their heads and scratching their brow, probably trying to absorb what they just saw.

It's about forty-five minutes until they finally bring the body out in a stretcher. Other motel guests watch from their rooms. The body has obviously been hacked up, because it doesn't look like a human body under the white sheet. Did the medics compile her dismembered to make it look like she was intact, or did they just throw all the pieces on the stretcher? It's sad to think how Tracey's loved ones will hear about this. I wonder if Tracey had loved ones?

It takes another twenty-five minutes until the police notice me across the street. Two of them, officers, approach my vehicle.

On "A Nation's Justice" yesterday, a show about how forensic-science helps solve cold cases, a detective talked about a suspect who became a suspect solely on the fact that he lied to police while being questioned. The reason the suspect lied was because he had marijuana in his procession and didn't want authorities to investigate. The detective said that if the suspect hadn't lied, they probably would've gone to the next suspect, solving the case much faster. The detective makes a critical point because lying to the authorities misleads them from the track they should be on. So I decide to tell them why I am here in my car. I tell them that I can see inside the killer's head. So sure enough, within ten minutes, I'm cuffed, stuffed in the back of a police car, and hauled into the police station.      I didn't really think this one through.

CHAPTER 13

# Interrogation

I'm in the interrogation room, swearing to myself that this is the last time I do the right thing. I wonder if they really think *I* did this. I wonder if they'll let me go.

Anger, bitterness and hopelessness brew. I'm feeling suicidal again. I often wonder how painful self-immolation is. I figure if I were to kill myself, I'd go out being remembered for dying the most painful way. People would say, "Shit, that guy really wanted to show how much pain he was willing to inflict on himself." But then again, burning alive isn't fool proof. You never know if someone will rescue you and then you walk around the rest of your life as a burn victim. That would suck. I assume the most painful way to kill yourself but most likely to be successful, is by drowning. I mean, no one can stop you from diving off a bridge with bricks tied around your feet. And even if they were to rescue you, you'd have brain damage by the time they got you out of the water. But, with my luck I'm sure I'll just kill myself by making my bed-sheets into a noose in my prison cell.

There is however, a little light when I am introduced to Detective George Curtis, whom I recognize from the newspapers and books I have been reading about the Seattle Slayer. Detective Curtis is a fat guy, about five foot nine or so, and has dark brown hair (probably dyed).

There is a mirror in the room. Someone is obviously recording me from the other side of it. I often look into it to see if I can tell how fucking scared I look.

There is a third person in the room. A young detective who is about my age and is almost as handsome as me. He shows me some respect, though I have none for him. I think he believes that I am not the Slayer. His name is Detective Marlon Lime. Lime. I like that name.

They ask me everything about everything. I tell them the lot truthfully and they still don't believe me. I told them about Yeval. The Pearl. The Dark Room. The yellow screen. The ruby. I even make the point that the Seattle Slayer was at large *before I was born!* All Lime says is, "Still, Randy, your position" meaning where I was parked "was awfully suspicious." What a faggot.

It takes Lime three hours to *finally* ask me if I am in therapy. I tell them, "Call up Dr. Jenkins. Dr. *Dwight* Jenkins."

"I need a breather," Curtis says casually, which makes me suspicious. I liked Curtis at first because I recognized him, but he seems like a prick now. I ought to beat his fat ass up, then maybe he will change his tone.

Curtis leaves, and his little lapdog Lime follows him. The door to the interrogation room closes and I am now isolated, trapped. The room is bright white, and I just know there's a camera on the opposite side of that mirror. This place is like the opposite of the Dark Room. This is the Light Room.

I wonder what my father would think of me right now?

I wish I could go back in time six hours. It's amazing how your life can change so quickly. I am hopeless.

I take a nap in the Light Room. I don't dream. I just lay my head on that cheap table, close my eyes, and rest.

"They think you did it." It's Yeval. He is sitting on the floor against the wall to my right.

I bring my head up and say, "Fuck you."

"You were an idiot for going to that motel," he says. "Now do you believe me?"

"Believe what?"

"That you can see through the killer's eyes!"

"You never told me that," I say, putting my head back down on the table, pretending not to have figured it out already.

"You knew it already," he says.

"So, what do you want?"

"Just to enjoy this moment. You will never see Ryan again. You will never fuck Morgan again. You will never make up with your father. You will never marry Caroline. You will never be a father. You are going away for the rest of your life."

I try to ignore him, but I'm getting pissed. It's what he wants.

Yeval picks at his long toe-nails and begins chuckling, "You just had to visit that motel. None of this would have happened if you just listened to me."

The door opens. God knows how long it's been since I've been in here. Lime and Curtis enter. To my surprise, Dr. Jenkins is with them.

"Who were you talking to, Randy?" Lime says condescendingly.

"Yeval," I say, looking at Dr. Jenkins. "He's here." I look over and notice Yeval is gone. Yeval usually blabbers while I'm trying to have a conversation with someone, rather than just disappear. I find it strange that he just left. For the first time, I am uncomfortable without him.

"Who is this Yeval?" Lime asks Dr. Jenkins, even though I mentioned Yeval a thousand fucking times to him already.

Before Dr. Jenkins answers (it even looks like Curtis is about to answer), someone else enters. It is a rather large man, wearing a police uniform. He has a caveman-brow which makes him look angry, but in his eyes I can tell this is a jolly man of good-temper. He carries a coffee mug. If he's in his late sixties he looks young for his age, if he's in his early fifties he has aged poorly. His ridiculous comb-over only makes his age that much more of a mystery.

"Randy, I'd like you to meet my long-time good friend," Dr. Jenkins introduces, "Chief Harold Milton. He is in charge of the Seattle Slayer case."

I stand up and shake his hand respectfully. Like Curtis, his name is mentioned in the books on Slayer as well.

"Hello Randy," says Chief, forcing a smile. He suspects me. I can tell.

I want to mention how I recognized his name from the Slayer books, but think that mentioning that I've "studied" the Seattle Slayer is suspicious, so I just say, "Nice to meet you, Chief." I follow it up with a smile.

Chief takes a seat across from me while Jenkins, Lime and Curtis remain standing. Chief opens a folder, slips on his glasses, and clicks his pen.

"Tell me everything you know about the recent Slayer killings, Randy," Chief says with no inflection, the feeling burnt out of his voice by the whole damn case.

"I know everything, beginning from the Sizemore family killed a few weeks ago," I respond, noticing Curtis's look to at Dr. Jenkins.

"Tell me what you know," Chief says while writing.

"I know that the Sizemore wife spit her teeth out of her mouth while Slayer was still standing over her," I respond.

"Go on," says the chief.

"The bat was first used to kill Mr. Sizemore."

"Yes," Chief says. I get the impression that he is not impressed with what I know because what I am describing to him is so vague. The newspapers reported that Mr. and Mrs. Sizemore were killed with a bat. And though the newspapers never said that Mr. Sizemore was killed first, or that his neck was broken, it's a logical conclusion. I realize I'm not telling them anything so I say something that will make them shit themselves.

"The Sizemore child wasn't killed with a bat," I say, thumbing the nail on my middle finger. I add in a quick mumble, "It was bleach that killed him."

Looking at my fingernail, I glance up at everyone in the room. They are all staring at me.

"How did you know that?" Chief asks suspiciously.

"Like I told you, I can see through the killer's eyes," I say. "I may be crazy, but I ain't a liar."

"Why did you do it!" Lime leaps forward, slamming his palm down on the table, trying to startle me.

"Detective Lime!" Chief turns over his shoulder. "You screamed right in my ear. Step back, and take your notes, kiddo. I'll do the talking."

Chief looks back at me. He thinks I did it. So does Lime. I assume Dr. Jenkins and Curtis both think I did this too, but they both remain quiet for the moment. My focus turns to how I am going to prove to them that I did not commit these murders. Why would they believe me?

"Tell me more, kid," says Chief.

I stare back at Chief Milton trying to decide on what the right thing to say is. "I want to go to the crime scene," I say.

"You're not allowed at the crime scene," Curtis chimes in.

"But psychic-detectives get to go to the crime-scene sometimes," I say. I don't expect them to let me go to one of the crime scenes. I don't know what I expect of them.

"You're not a psychic-detective," says Lime.

I have come to realize that the truth as I know it is so far fetched, the detectives won't even believe me with Dr. Jenkins on my side. There is no way to prove myself to them. I have no say in the Light Room just like I have no say in the Dark Room. But, if I can get out of the Dark Room, I can get out of the Light Room. There is only one way to get out of this interrogation, as well as get out of being a suspect. I have to go to my jail cell and wait for Slayer to strike again. I have to sit through everything in the Dark Room so I can prove that I know every detail of the murder, a virtually impossible task except for in this particular circumstance.

"I like to shove garden-hoses in whore's pussies," I say unrepentantly. "It gets me off."

"Would you like to speak with your lawyer, Mr. Mulray," Lime says.

"What does he need a lawyer for?" Dr. Jenkins breaks in. "The kid is thirty-years too young to be the fucking killer. You have the wrong suspect."

Chief Milton turns around. "He knows undisclosed information. That makes him a suspect." He's goaded by the presence of Jenkins.

I am aware that Slayer did leave behind usable DNA evidence in previous crimes. There is just nobody to link it to. This is also undisclosed information they don't dare mention to me because they don't want me to know. But I already know. "Do a DNA test," I persuade, hoping this shows them I don't give a shit about any of this.

"We will, don't you worry," says Lime, even though I wasn't fucking talking to him.

"I wasn't fucking talking to you, faggot," I say.

Curtis laughs at the fact that I called his partner a faggot. Lime laughs because I just dug myself deeper in the shit. I laugh proudly at how cool I know I am. Chief and Dr. Jenkins don't laugh.

"That's it, I've had enough," says Chief Milton angrily, even though I know he knows I didn't do this. "We're holding you, and we are going to request no bail." Punishment.

"Yes, your honor," I say.

Chief closes the file, looks at me, and then looks away rolling his eyes. Dr. Jenkins is giving me the same look. The two men, who are both wise and good-hearted, are disappointed in me because they know I'm better than this. I know I'm better than this too. As I'm being escorted out of the Light Room by two faggoty deputies, I myself wonder why I get a rise out of digging myself deeper into holes. Why am I being a smartass?

Dr. Jenkins doesn't get a chance to talk to me before I get locked up in the jail cell. But I know I'll be seeing more of him soon.

That night, the jail cell is completely empty for forty-five minutes. During this short period of privacy, I decide to take a shit. I notice that some lowlife cummed under the toilet seat. I laughed. I become so bored and horny in my cell, I decided to crawl into the corner and attempt to perform fellatio on myself just to pass time. I have heard my friends talk about trying to perform fellatio on themselves, but I had never tried until now. I'm a very flexible person but I still can't reach. I was disappointed that I wasn't man enough to reach my own dick with my mouth, but then again I was very relieved that I didn't suck my own dick out of sheer boredom.

A bum and a Mexican enter the cell around the same time. The Mexican looks dangerous but he probably couldn't take me. He doesn't even attempt to pull any shit. The bum however is a pervert and wants to know if I was "down doin' da II", and I told him to give his father a rim job.

After a couple hours I begin crying about the fact that I'm locked up again. The thing that gets me down the most is that my mother is dead, my brother is retarded, my relationship with my father is in the gutter, and worst of all is that all of this is my fault. I cry helplessly, and I assume that the other guys watching (even the weirdo taking a shit in front of everybody) think I'm a pathetic crybaby.

Rumor in the cell is that it's already 2:30am. No sign of Yeval.

CHAPTER 14

# Noon

It has been over a day since my arrest and the judge set bail at five million dollars. I wonder if Asshole will come to bail me out.

I met this lawyer, who's name I didn't bother to remember. The city appointed him to me because I don't have an income (I do, the police just don't know about it). My lawyer is a smooth talker but he isn't nearly as suave as me. He's surely not suave enough to prove to a dog that I didn't commit these murders. I'm not relying on him to get out of here. Instead I'm relying on Yeval and Slayer, my two worst enemies.

I met up with my lawyer this morning. I didn't speak much to him, and didn't listen to anything he had to say. I remember him telling me, "You have to talk to me if you want me to help you," to which I responded, "I'm kind of drained, if you don't mind." He's a chubby short guy with glasses, maybe even younger than me.

Breakfast this morning was four fresh carrot-sticks, four scrumptious celery-sticks served with a choice of blue-cheese dressing or peanut-butter, and a two day old blueberry muffin made from *real* blueberries! I was so pissed, I didn't even eat it. I took the paper plate with the bullshit excuse for a breakfast and said to the person (cook? officer? don't give a shit) serving it to me, "Is this a fucking joke?" Then, like a spoiled child, I threw the plate to the floor. The officer made me clean it up—and I don't want to talk about it anymore. I'm still tough because I haven't eaten in nearly day and I am purposely trying to beat my record of four-days straight, which I set when I was twelve.

Right now I am sitting on a concrete bench in the cell with six other guys. I pass the time by picking my toe jam. It smells like pickles. I'm not weird enough to taste it. I sat down on the bench because I popped a boner when I was thinking about how big Morgan's titties are and how nice it would be to fuck and cum all over them again. The thought of my mother pops in my head and I begin to get depressed again. Before my eyes tear up, I hear somebody say, "Is the little baby going to cry?"

My bare feet, now all clean of toe-jam, are cris-crossed. I uncross them, put them on the freezing pavement and stand up.

"Who the fuck said that?" I say. I look around, only four out of the six guys give me their attention. I give them a minute to answer. Nobody does, and they all look away. "Who the fuck said that?" I say again, adding, "was it you?" I walk up to a guy in his mid-thirties, taller than me, buffer than me, but not as handsome as me, and grab him by the shirt with one hand and pull him up to my face. "What did you say!" I repeat angrily, my dilated pupil glaring at him.

"Chill!" the guy says. "I didn't say shit."

"What's your problem, dude?," another guy says. "You're the first person to say anything in the last hour."

"Oh," I say, letting go out the other guy. I try flattening the wrinkles I made on his shirt. "Sorry." I smile and blush in embarrassment. "I'll buy you a burger."

The guy looks away, confused and scared. I hear a laugh from behind me. I defensively turn around and see that nobody is laughing. "Yeval," I say to myself. Sure enough, when I look more closely, there is the Pearl floating in the middle of the cell. I grab it.

I take a seat in the red chair. The yellow curtain has already been pulled. As the lights dim, Yeval whispers to me, "How's prison?"

"Hasn't changed," I respond, looking underneath my chair for the ruby. It isn't there, and fear flows through my body.

It's late afternoon as Slayer stands in the backyard of a three-story white house. A gorgeous housewife has her back turned to him. He is peeking through rows of hanging cloths. The housewife is washing them manually, soaking t-shirts in a basket.

Slayer creeps forward, slowly revealing a bicycle chain. He's about three feet behind her when he finally gets her attention by swirling his left foot around in the damp grass, making a squeaking sound. The housewife (who I would love to fuck) turns around to see a bicycle chain meeting the left side of her forehead.

She falls to the ground, holding her face with both hands. She doesn't cry. She doesn't scream. She doesn't even moan. She rolls around helplessly on the grass, her bare-toes squeezing down hard enough to pull grass from the ground.

She squirms around for about thirty seconds. Slayer crushes her ribs with his foot and kicks her in the spine. She freezes in surrender as he lays on top of her. She suddenly snaps into defensive mode when he attempts to hold her shoulders down with his legs. She screams, "Fire" loudly repeatedly, while pulling on his crotch area. I hear him moan in pain while she has a grip on his nut-sack. He has enough control to wrap the bicycle-chain around her neck. All the while, she's screaming at the top of her lungs and getting close to popping one of his balls.

He begins to strangle. Her loud cries of, "Fire," begin to fade but her jaw remains open. As I look into her dying eyes, pooling in blood, I am reminded of Munch's "The Scream".

A thick vein running down her forehead swells, as both sides of her temples begin to bloat. Sweat drips from her pours and her skin turns purple. She is dead after thirty seconds, but Slayer still squeezes her neck until both her eyes pop out of their sockets; the left eye first, then the right. The screen fades and I am back in the jail cell.

I look around at the six men surrounding me. They don't even notice that I just came back from a different world, dimension, whatever.

About four hours later, an officer approaches the cell. "Randy Mulray," he says. I walk up to the barred-door. The officer opens the door. I put my wrists together expecting to be cuffed, but instead the guard tells me to follow.

I walk behind him into the chief's office, where Chief is watching "breaking news on television." Reading glasses sit on his clean and tidy desk, and a folder with a mug-shot of me when I was seventeen next to his glasses. Chief is standing, his back to the entrance, frozen with his mouth covered. Though his back is turned to me I can still see his face. His face is red in frustration, his eyes swollen with tears.

I can sense the frustration and sadness this man must be feeling. Year after year of hard work, and there is no progress. I can relate to this kind of failure. For the first time in my life I can read through somebody's eyes. Deep down he knows I didn't do it, and he's coming to terms with that. I'm sure his guilt augments for putting me, an already fucked up person, into this fucked up situation.

My plan to prove myself had worked, but it was done in vain. I had to let another innocent victim fall into the hands of a ruthless killer so I could prove my point. I realize now that my life is not worth saving like those of the Sizemore family, the housewife, Tracy, Jason Ramsey, and all the other victims. The unpleasant and undeserving live longer, and I am among them. I would rather spend the rest of my useless, selfish, wasteful life in jail, rather than let another Slayer murder occur. But that is beyond my control. I gain more of an understanding of Chief Milton as he does me. We both see that two completely different people have more in common than the others closest to us. Chief Milton is haunted by the Seattle Slayer, as I am haunted by Yeval.

I am free man again. But I feel no better.

"Tell me everything, Randy," Chief Milton says. "Everything."

CHAPTER 15

# Investigation

After running Chief through what I know of the housewife's murder, whose name is Linda Herman, he calls detective George Curtis and Marlon Lime, both of whom have the day off, so the four of us can look over a couple of the crime scenes together.

I haven't been home in a couple of days. My stomach grumbles for a decent meal. I didn't get to shower either.

As we walk to the exit, Chief Milton says to me, "Randy, reporters are swarming the building. Don't say anything. They are going to ask you if all charges have been dropped."

"Have they?"

"Yes," answers Lime.

Chief continues, "Don't tell them that we are taking you to a crime scene."

"If I'm not supposed to be there, then why am I going?" I ask.

"Good question," Curtis says.

Chief explains, "We *need* you. If you're useless to us at the crime scene, we'll let you go. But I think you're the key to the identity of the Seattle Slayer."

We exit the station, and immediately (just like in the movies), reporters run toward the four of us with microphones, some with just notepads, as cameras flash.

I ignore the reporters and try to continue the conversation with Chief. "So, like a psychic detective?" I ask curiously, knowing that's what he's using me for.

Lime, Curtis and Chief all simultaneously shush me.

"Just don't speak," Curtis barks.

We get in the car, I get shotgun, and we drive off.

***

On the way there, very little conversation is exchanged:

"I just want to see if you can help," Chief Milton.

"PDs are useless, unreliable, and a waste of time," Detective Curtis, slowly becoming more and more of a prick. "This is bullshit."

"No psychic has ever been given official recognition from the F.B.I. But it will be interesting to see what's on your mind," Detective Marlon Lime who is surprisingly becoming more and more nice.

"Do you guys drink lots of coffee and eat a lot of donuts?" me.

\*\*\*

Chief, pulls into a parking garage on 10<sup>th</sup> and Macy, at the Moore Building. He pulls up to the guy at the ticket booth. Chief whips out his badge like a fucking V.I.P pass, and the guy lets us through.

We keep driving until we reach floor E. Chief parks the car and the four of us get out.

The parking space three spots to the right of where we're parked, I can see faint brownish-colored stains. The three watch as I take a closer look. I kneel down and see little strand-patterns in the stain.

"This is a blood stain," I say.

I point and then turn around to look at them.

"No shit," says Detective Curtis.

"There are markings in the stains. It's from Ramsey's hair," I say. "When his skin was ripped off his neck, blood encircled around his head."

"Yes, Ramsey's body was found upright. But there were no stains from his hair," says Curtis. "Give me a break. Besides, even if there was, the prints wouldn't still be here after the blood was scrubbed out."

"Come on, Randy," says Chief. "I'm giving you a chance to prove yourself."

A few inches to the right I see, very pale, "SLAYER" written next to the stain.

"Fuck," I say to myself as I trace it with my finger. "Far out."

"Fuck this shit," says Curtis.

"Randy. This isn't the crime scene," says Chief.

"This is just where some punk kids recreated the crime scene with food-coloring and corn-syrup," says Curtis. "One hundred hours of community service for them when they got caught."

I look at the big E on the wall and realize it was floor C that I remember from what I originally saw in the Dark Room.

"This isn't the right floor," I say.

"Very good. Way to realize that after we told you it wasn't the crime scene," says Curtis. "You're full of shit."

"Come on, let's go," Chief says.

"No," I beg. "I'm telling you the truth. Shit. I knew you wouldn't believe me."

"Wait," says Lime.

"What?" Curtis asks.

"How would Randy know that the victim's skin was torn from the neck?" asks Lime.

"So?" says Curtis.

"This wasn't in any newscast or article I know of. All the public knows is that Jason Ramsey was stabbed in the neck. Nothing else," Lime points out.

"Randy," says Chief Milton. "What weapon did Slayer stab the victim in the neck with?"

"A piece of shattered glass," I immediately reply.

"He also knew that the victim was laying upright," says Lime.

"Nothing more than a fifty-fifty guess," says Curtis. "The victim was either found face down or face up. Big fucking deal."

"But the victim being stabbed in the neck with glass?" says Chief. "How would Randy know that?"

"Has your brain shrunken overnight, Harold?" Curtis says angrily. "He's obviously involved. No other way."

"But isn't it a little too convenient, if I *were* the killer, to copy Slayer's exact profile?"

"It's even more convenient you see this shit in your head," Curtis replies.

"But if I were a copycat killer, I'd be much less experienced of a killer than Slayer is, so you could assume I'd be more nervous."

"I guess," Curtis crosses his arms as he replies.

"Breaking a window, luring a stranger, and killing him with the glass from the broken window, in a public place, is pretty risky for a copycat killer," I say.

"Risky, unlikely, but not impossible," Chief interrupts.

"I proved myself as much as I could," I say to Chief. "I'm not doing it anymore. You wouldn't have dragged me out to some parking garage if you thought I was dangerous. Nope. If you really thought I was dangerous, you would've done everything in your power to keep me behind bars."

"Plus, he's admitting more to us than any guilty person would," says Lime. "If he really did it, why would he be telling us this?"

"That's exactly what you wants us to think," says Curtis.

Curtis points his finger at me. What a dork.

"Slayer asked Ramsey if he could use a cell-phone to call the police, claiming his window has been broken," I say. "Ramsey gave him his cell. Slayer calls 911, but *after* he maces and stabs Ramsey."

Chief stares at me insecurely.

"Should I continue?" I ask him.

"No," he says. "Let's go."

"That's almost like a confession," says Curtis to Chief. "We gonna arrest him."

"I don't want to hear your shit right now, George," yells Chief.

Lime cracks a smile.

"Let's go, everyone," says Chief.

Chief gets in the car and slams the door shut.

"So, why was the skin torn on Ramsey's neck if he was already dead from the glass wound?" Lime asks me as I walk by him.

"When Slayer stabbed Ramsey…" I whisper, making sure that Curtis, who is trying to listen, can't hear.

"Yeah?" says Lime.

"The force was so strong that it dug right into it his neck without drawing a single drop of blood," I continue. "The torn skin was out of frustration. Slayer couldn't write his signature without drawing the victim's blood."

"Get in, faggots," Curtis yells at me.

In the car, Curtis whispers, "I got my eye on you. If you know what's best for you, go away."

\*\*\*

Curtis doesn't say shit to me for the rest of the drive. In fact, he didn't even join us in the Sizemore house to hear what I have to say.

"All bullshit," is what I hear him mumble to Lime as the three of us get out of the car when we arrived at the Sizemores'.

Chief, Lime and I walk up the gravel path leading to the front porch. A sign reading "DO NOT ENTER" hangs on the door.

"Why is this area still undisclosed, but the parking garage wasn't?" I ask them.

"We got about forty-eight hours to get all the evidence from the crime scene, in public areas," Lime responds. "The Sizemores owned this house, so in this case, we can close this area off much much longer."

"Oh," I say.

Chief and Lime walk up the stands. I stand at the bottom.

"What?" asks Lime.

"Is it possible to go through the back instead?" I ask.

Lime looks at Chief.

"Sure," Chief says.

We walk around the back to the patio. I look in through the broken kitchen window. Clear plastic covers the holes in the window. The breeze constantly blows the plastic inward.

This is what I saw in the Dark Room. The image is exactly the same.

The fact that I am actually here suddenly creeps me greatly. There are tingles throughout my body that I have never felt before.

I fall to the ground.

"Whoa!" Lime shrieks.

Both Chief and Lime immediately come to aid me.

Within a second of the fall, I get back up, with Chief and Lime assisting me about halfway.

"Are you okay?" Chief asks.

"I feel fine."

I really do.

"Let's go inside," I say.

"You sure?" Chief asks.

"Yeah."

I walk Chief and Lime through what I *saw* happen. I think I actually get Lime's faith when I point out where Mrs. Sizemore spit out her teeth after being knocked in the head. The entire time, they listen to everything I say without interrupting or asking questions. We are out of there within fifteen minutes.

I find it very logical that Lime and Chief suspect I had some part in this as well. But they can't prove anything, because there is no proof I did it.

I'll to continue to tell the truth; I don't care how crazy I sound. It's my turn to take advantage of Yeval. As my mother always said, *the truth will lead to an end*. I know the truth, so I can put a stop to the Seattle Slayer.

As much as I don't want to, I am going to keep going into the Dark Room in order to know everything there is to know. I am going to be a psychic detective. I don't care how crazy and unrealistic that sounds. I know I'm a reliable source, and I know now that I can use this curse of mine as a gift to put one the most notorious serial killer away.

Chief Milton drops me off at my apartment complex. He makes an attempt to get to know me. He asks me where I went to school, if I have a girlfriend or children, how long I have had these images, if he has my permission to talk to Dr. Jenkins about my situation, and other get-to-know-you questions. He's probably building a read on me in order to find cracks in my story.

I thank him for the ride. As his car pulls into the Seattle traffic, I get the feeling this isn't the last I'll hear from Chief Milton. How do I know? Chief and Lime believe, and they'll want more info.

In celebration of being released from prison, pouring my knowledge into the hands of the people who have been trying to put a serial killer away, and an epiphany that Yeval may be a gift, I decide to jump into my car and drive to Caroline's.

# CHAPTER 16

# Caroline

I stand at the bottom of the stairs at Caroline's apartment complex. Overwhelmed with happiness, I almost don't want to see Caroline because I'm afraid something bad might happen to ruin the good feeling I rarely get. I can't remember the last time I felt so happy.

I look up the stairs and choke on my breath when I realize that I haven't been here in years. It seems like just yesterday. My right foot takes the first step. Memories of Caroline and me snuggling together as we watch movies roll through my mind.

When I finally reach the top of the second floor, guilt washes over me when I remember grabbing Caroline by her arms and screaming in her face. I remember that I got so angry with her over her smacking me (which I did deserve), that I almost hit her back. If I were to hit her back, she could have been seriously injured...because I am so strong. I never wanted to hurt or scare the most precious thing in my life.

I broke it off because I was scared for her. I was scared of me and I didn't want her to get hurt. I couldn't trust myself.

I walk my way to the door, my happiness overwhelmed by regret. I exhale deeply. Why am I doing this?

"Can I answer it, Mommy?" I hear a little girl say after I knock on the door.

Shit, what's Caroline's little girl's name again? Janelle? No. I know it starts with a J though. Jenny? No. Jane? No. Jessica? Yeah, I think that's it.

She answers the door.

"Hi Jessica!" I say enthusiastically.

"My name is Jane."

Damn it!

"Is your mommy or daddy home?"

"I don't live with my daddy."

77

This girl is adorable. She has blue eyes like her mother, brown hair unlike her mother, and is wearing purple overalls which are just so cute.

"Mom," she yells. "It's not grandma."

"Well of course I'm your grandma," I say to her in an old lady voice. "Don't you recognize me?"

"No!" she giggles. "You're not my grandma! You're young and you're a *boy.*"

Caroline pulls the door open.

"Randy!" Caroline exclaims, smiling.

"Hey Caroline," I say, trying not to blush.

"I expected you to call. Come in."

Yes! I walk in to Caroline's apartment, which has seen a lot of work, but still smells the same. Jane closes the door behind me.

"Thank you, little lady," I say to Jane.

"Jane, this is my old friend Randy," Caroline says to her daughter.

"Like Randy from class?" Jane asks.

"Yeah, like Randy from class," Caroline confirms.

"I'm three," says Jane to me.

"Three! How many is that?" I say, holding out four fingers faking my knowledge of numbers.

"No!" Jane says, laughing. "This many!"

She holds up three fingers.

"Ooh, that's a lot," I say, pretending to be impressed. "You're a big girl."

"Honey, why don't you go back to drawing," Caroline tells Jane.

Jane runs upstairs, waving goodbye. I wave back to her. I watch the cute little thing run upstairs and then look to Caroline's beautiful blue eyes. Caroline stares at me without blinking. I can't read her emotion. I never could. It's what always attracted me to her. I dig the mystery.

There is a long moment of silence. Astonishment still flows through her body, making her speechless. Either that or she's nervous. She's chewing gum with her mouth open and blinks numerously.

"It's so weird to be back in this room," I say.

She nods and smiles.

"I'm sorry if I interrupted your time with your daughter." I can't think of anything else to say.

"No, no, no. It's okay," she tells me. "I thought you were my mother, who's supposed to be here to pick her up."

"Where are you going?"

"Just to Portland for a day and a half on business."

Another knock comes from the door.

"Excuse me," she goes to answer.

"Is that Grandma?" Jane says, peaking out over the stair handle.

"Yes," Caroline says. "Jane! Get off that stair handle, you're going to fall. Go get your backpack."

Jane runs down the stairs with a little pink backpack already on, rushes past the two of us, and answers the door.

Even more old memories rush through my head when I see Caroline's mother.

"Randy!" Caroline's mother says to me, not even acknowledging her granddaughter.

"Hey, Betty," I say shyly, embarrassed for some reason.

"How are you?" she asks.

"Grandma, Grandma, Grandma," Jane says, trying to get her attention by jumping up and down.

"I'm dong fine. You?" I respond.

Caroline walks over and unzips Jane's backpack which is still on her back. "Okay, you got everything Jane?"

"Have a good trip, sweetie," Caroline's mother says to her. Caroline's mother kisses Caroline on her cheek.

"I will," Caroline says. "You be good for Grandma," she turns to Jane.

"I will," Jane says, and kisses Caroline on the cheek.

It's quite eerie because they all look alike, yet they are all completely different. Caroline must have looked like Jane when she was little and she'll probably look like her mother when she is older. The sight is simply beautiful.

"I'll see you two," Caroline says. "Thanks for taking Jane."

"Have a good trip," Caroline's mother says. "It was nice seeing you again, Randy. I was afraid I was never going to see you anymore."

"It was nice seeing you too," I say.

The door closes, and Caroline and I are standing together in the room we used to make love in. It was on a corduroy-blue couch still sitting in the same place we last made love. I fear she may have had sex with other men on that couch too, but I have no right to be jealous.

"So, what brings you by?" she asks, still happy but tired of wondering what brought me here.

"I wasn't feeling well," I say.

I wonder if that was the right thing to say.

"Well, how can I help?"

She smiles and tilts her head. She looks deep into my eyes, knowing something is bothering me. I'm sure she has a few assumptions, and I can tell she's very curious.

"I already feel better," I say.

Yeah! Perfect answer. That was awesome! What is she gonna do now?

She laughs.

"Can I get you a drink?" she says, heading over to the kitchen.

"No thanks, don't bother," I say, even though I could use one after all the shit I've been through.

"Well," she begins, having no clue what to say, "I'm driving to Portland, so I can stick around for a few more hours. I mean, it's not like I have to catch a flight."

I don't know what to say.

"Okay. Let's sit down," she says, placing her hand on my muscular shoulder, guiding me to the couch. As we sit, she asks with sudden concern, "So, is it anything serious?"

"When you and I were together," I sigh, preparing to spill my guts, "I used to have this *thing* that used to taunt me. Yeval."

"I remember," she says.

I realize that I have mentioned Yeval to her before, though I can't remember the circumstance. I imagine she caught me talking to nobody, and I told her. Oh well.

"Do you remember Yeval telling me to do bad things?"

"What kind of bad things?" she asks.

She's speaking softly; I can tell she's at ease.

"Bad things. Very bad things," I confess. "Sick, disgusting, cruel things."

"Okay."

"Yeval used to tell me to kill people," I say, knowing that there is no turning back. If Caroline understands me, I am going to marry her. If she doesn't understand me, I am going to kill myself. "People I loved. He'd tell me how to take advantage of Ryan, or give me reasons to kill my father. I remember one night when we were sleeping together, I woke up to find Yeval telling me how easy it would be to snap your neck while you were asleep. He'd list off reasons why I should do it."

Caroline sits back, not knowing what to think.

I continue. "I broke up with you because when I was extremely angry with you, I felt this unimaginable fury. I was afraid I would do what Yeval was urging me to do. I didn't want to hurt you. You were the most important thing to me. I wanted you to be safe from someone like me."

I take a breath, giving her time to absorb.

"I was a suspect in the Slayer killings," I tell her. "*Was* a suspect. *Was*."

I look up at her, ashamed of myself.

"But, in the five years we've been apart, I haven't hurt a fly. I haven't had the urge to hurt anything. And I haven't stopped thinking about you either. I discovered how I can control Yeval.

"There is more I need to work on. None of it may ever be perfect. But I figure I owe it to you to tell you everything and let you know that I met hundreds of women since we were together, and none of them are half the person you are. I have never found anything more beautiful in my life.

"If I had only one wish—with all the fucked up problems I have, I could use more than one. But, if I had only one wish, I'd wish to be with you forever."

I stare into her beautiful eyes, praying that she knows how truthful I am being.

"You don't have to wish, Randy," she says, putting your hand on mine.

"What?" I'm stunned. "How can you possibly understand and believe me after all the crazy shit I just told you, and all the bullshit I put you through?"

"I know you too well," she says. "I know that you lead an unusual and sad life. But it amazes me how caring, truthful and loving you are. You told me that breaking up was for my benefit. Though I didn't understand it, I believed that's what you believed. No person has ever looked out for me or shown me as much love as you. I know it's genuine and that's all I need. I trust you won't hurt me. I don't care what Yeval tells you, and I don't care what you fear. I know what you're capable of."

Without hesitation, I push my mouth against hers. Our lips touch.

I open my eyes and see that her eyes are closed. My fingers crawl through her dark blonde her, and my fingertips brush it back. I smell strawberries. She still uses the same shampoo. I smile, my lips still gripping onto hers, and I gently grab her tender arms, press my chest against hers, and softly lay her down as I slowly come down on top of her.

"I missed you so, my Caroline," I whisper softly, as my hands run down her arms and hold her hands.

I nibble on her neck and let her hands go free, both of which immediately cling to the back of my head, scratching and burying me deeper into her neck. My hands reach up the bottom of her shirt and under to bra. I feel her bare-breasts, cupping them with my hands, squeezing them gently and pushing them together softly. My thumbs rub her nipples as my lips dig deeper into her neck.

I slowly begin thrusting as I continue to kiss her neck and play with her nipples. When I hear her release an short moan, I release my hands from her breast and move down to her inner thigh. I move my hand up to the top of her pants, slowly unbuckling her belt and unsnap her jeans. She doesn't stop me. I push my fingertips under her soft cotton panties, and glide them over her trimmed (but not shaven) pubic hair.

I touch her vagina. There is so much cunt—I mean vaginal-fluid—I easily insert my index and middle fingers in. As I'm fingering her, I lift my head from her neck and kiss her again. Our tongues wrestle aggressively.

I pull my fingers out of her, and pull her pants off with both of my hands. She looks up into my eyes and spreads her legs open, showing me her wet vulva. I lay on top of her again, kissing her passionately and pulling my own pants down at the same time.

The base of my erect penis accidentally rubs up against her labia. I am expecting her to stop us because she either doesn't feel comfortable or because I don't have a condom. But she doesn't. She grabs on to my penis and puts it in.

I move my lips back down to her neck as I thrust into her making her moan again. I run my tongue all over her neck, as she moans, "Oh yeah Randy," continuously. I grip on to her tender ass and squeeze it hard. I grip it firmly so I am able to hump her hard.

I pull out as I am about to cum, but she tells me that she wants more. She guides my penis back in. The touch of her hand on my throbbing penis almost makes me ejaculate, but I don't. About to cum, I pull out again and take my shirt off. Then takes her shirt off too and I unsnap her bra.

I suck on her left tit as I squeeze the right.

"I want more," she begs.

I flip her on top of me, and she guides my penis back into her.

I grab her ass again and begin humping softly, pacing myself. I pull her close enough to where I can suck her titties while I fuck her. I suck on them hard, and bite gently.

"I'm gonna fucking cum!" I shout.

She pushes my head, still sucking on her left tit, down to the pillow, and digs her fingernails into my shoulder. She feels my muscles as her eyes roll back and moans in her beautiful feminine voice, "Oh yeah." I squirt a quick, but an amazingly thick load.

What Morgan and I have is sex.

This is love.

This was the first time I made love to someone in a while. I love her and she still loves me. I suppose I am very lucky. It was the best two minutes of my life.

CHAPTER 17

# Mall

I am walking out of Best Buy, where I just spent over three-hundred dollars on CD's. I could have borrowed them from the library like I usually do, but I was at the mall buying Panda Express and for some reason got the urge to buy CD's. The CD's I bought today were: "God Shuffled His Feet" by Crash Test Dummies, "Exile on Main Street" by The Rolling Stones, "Moondance" by Van Morrison, "The Slim Shady LP" by Eminem, "One Night Only" by Elton John, "Natty Dread" by Bob Marley, "The World is Yours" by Scarface, "Be Here" by Keith Urban, "Screamadelica" by Primal Scream, "Fat of the Land" and "Music for the Jilted Generation" both by The Prodigy, "Jar of Flies" by Alice in Chains, "Rearviewwindow" by Pearl Jam, "Sgt. Pepper's Lonely Hearts Club Band" by The Beatles, and "Stunt" by Barenaked Ladies.

I'm familiar with most of these albums and have heard all of them at least twice before, but I just needed to have them in my album collection. I have over 750 albums now; only 200 have been burnt from the library.

Caroline gets back in town today and I want to have a mix ready by the time her flight arrives. I know I could use a file-sharing program to make her a mix like the rest of the world does, but I choose not to because there is a chance the .mp3 file I download could be of low quality and/or incomplete. Yes, it's unlikely, but I wouldn't dare take the risk of a poor quality track for a mix I'm giving Caroline. I used to make mixes for Caroline all the time when we were together and think it would be a nice surprise to make her a new one that I put a lot of work into. I am going to have a CD insert, writing a paragraph for each track as to why this song relates to us or reminds me of her. I know she loves Queen's "You're My Best Friend" and Derek & The Dominos "Layla", so those must be included on the mix.

I just got done working out at Xclusive. My muscles are bulging, and I am wearing a tank-top that shows off my ripped biceps.

I'm sitting at a table in the food-court, eating chow-mien with chop-sticks while I unwrap the CD's I just bought. Some hot bitch in her late teens (16 or 17) approaches me. God, I'd like to lick her tight pussy. She gives me a piece of paper with "Cindi (206) 663-0372" written on it.

I look up at the little cunt sprayed with despicably tacky grapefruit perfume. She says to me, "My friend thinks you're cute. Here's her number."

I don't saying anything.

The bitch stands there blankly, and then turns around and walks away fully confused. She walks over to a table nearby where an even hotter little slut is sitting. I'd like to squeeze those titties while fucking her virgin asshole. The cunt looks up at me and smiles. I grab my shit and leave immediately.

I enter a Rite Aide, one that I have been barred from, and buy an Aero Hair Shaver, and a pack of double-A batteries.

I walk back out to the food-court, where I see the two little cunts polishing off a cinnamon roll they are sharing. I guess the two are still at an I-wanna-act-like-a-lesbian-but-I-am-really-straight stage.

I hide in a corner as I load two batteries into the shaver. I click the on-switch and the shaver starts buzzing. I hold tight to my Best Buy bag. I sprint down the food-court holding the shaver out, and run up to "Cindi" and skim the shaver over her scalp. Her beautiful hair, that I am sure she just got dressed, falls into her lap.

"Life should not be a breeze for you just because you're beautiful!" I scream so loud, that I am out of breath.

I smash the shaver to the ground and run out of the mall.

At home, I narrow the forty-eight songs I chose for Caroline's mix down to twenty.

I turn on the television and find another special on the Seattle Slayer. This special talks about the gaps in-between victims. One reporter states, "The Seattle Slayer has become less motivated as time goes on. His lust for victims is increasing, but his taste is becoming less and less *interesting*. From supermodels to housewives. From police officers to construction workers. Slayer doesn't care who he kills anymore. Now it's anybody. Interesting or not. It's already been six days since his last victim. The people await his next move."

Morgan comes home from a long day of doing nothing and begins complaining about something I don't bother caring about. She tries to talk over the Slayer program, but I do a great job of blocking her out. Once a commercial comes, I am forced to listen to her though.

"I don't even consider that action-packed," she says, I assume she's talking about a movie. "I mean, only six people died. I wanted my ten dollars back, but the manager wouldn't give it to me."

I'm side-tracked again when the television airs a promo for yet another Seattle Slayer special.

"Ooh," Morgan says, tuning in. "I'd love it if there was a Seattle Slayer movie! Now that would be entertaining. Randy, why don't they have a Seattle Slayer movie?"

"Because they have no way to end it. Duh. He's still at large."

"That's what would make it so crazy though!" Morgan says, thinking she's realized something brilliant. "'He's still out there'!"

"Yeah, that's a good idea," I say sarcastically, though she doesn't sense it.

The program comes back on. I tune Morgan out while she's babbling, and watch archive news-footage from back in the seventies of the Seattle Slayer.

"What is this?" she asks me, looking at my computer.

I don't notice that Morgan is reading the heart-felt, passionate inserts I wrote for Caroline's CD.

"What is this shit, Randy?"

The document reads, "The piano exit to this song (Layla) is the most beautiful piece of music I have ever heard. It always reminded me of two people making passionate love to each other. When I hear this instrumental section, I imagine you walking me through a wooden gate to a cottage by a creek where we spend the rest of our lives together, here, the hereafter and after."

Shit. Caught? Nah.

"Don't look at that. It's a mix I am making for you," I say.

I get up and poke her playfully away from the computer screen. Luckily, I didn't type "Mix for Caroline" yet or I would have been busted. But then again, would I care? How many guys has Morgan fucked since we've been together? Six? Seven? At least five that I know of. I should probably dump the useless bitch right now. But I don't, and I don't know why.

On the television is a sketch of a Mexican guy whom a jogger (how typical) claimed to see exiting a crime scene in the early seventees (Slayer's second to last spree before his twenty year retirement). One of the interviewees marks the fifth person I heard in my research say, "I think it would be a nice twist if the Slayer turned out to be a minority or a woman. Maybe even a homosexual. Best of all! A minority lesbian!" No.

"Ooh, would you like to see me with another woman?" Morgan says, overhearing the television program. She is trying to turn me on, but she doesn't know that I think threesomes are too slutty. She should just do porn, while she still has the body for it.

"What songs do you have on my mix, Randy," she gets sidetracked. It isn't her CD. She doesn't deserve a CD. I think I will just burn a half Pink Floyd and half Elton John mix and tell her I put a lot of work into it, just to shut the bitch up. God, I hope she didn't give me an STD. Luckily, I'm smart enough to have never fucked her without a condom. Though I do eat her pussy frequently, I don't have herpes. I wonder if you could get HIV from eating a bitch out. God, she's so beautiful on the outside, but on the inside...on the inside I fear she may be crawling with something. Maybe even a fetus that isn't mine. Now, why doesn't Slayer just kill her? She deserves to die. Not these poor people that the television portrays as weak rather than helpless. If the media is going to portray a victim as weak rather than a FREAKIN' VICTIM then maybe it should be Morgan who dies. Maybe I should kill her. Maybe I should get a taste of that nice ass one last time, suck on the huge beautiful breasts of hers, and then shove my gat in her mouth and pull the fucking trigger. That way I can be with Caroline forever.

CHAPTER 18

# Hospital

I have been in the hospital for nearly a week recovering from an attack
I can barely remember. Car chases, car crashes, blood and rain-drops are all
I can recall from the night I was assaulted.

I woke from a "fifty-three hour coma", according to Dr. Sherman. I
have a few scars surrounding both eye-brows. My pinky toe is missing. According to Dr. Sherman, I'm lucky to be alive. An elderly couple found my
unconscious body hanging out of the broken windshield.

I had a splitting headache when I came out of the coma. My father
and brother were in the room watching a Mariner's game.

Caroline came to visit and so did Morgan. They ran into each other
Caroline later tells me. Although Asshole knows that I'm banging Caroline, I don't think Morgan knows (or cares). Investigators come to ask me
questions twice. Detective Lime and Curtis also stopped in to ask me questions. Perhaps they think I was assaulted by Slayer?

The last clear memory I have was driving to Louis, my drug-supplier.
I told Louis I was dropping by to pick up more dope, when actually I was
on my way to Louis's to let him know in person that I was done with the
drug-business. I barely even do drugs so what's the point in me selling
them? If I remember correctly, things got out of hand. They might have
chopped my pinky toe off, maybe attempted to stab me, but somehow
I must have gotten away. My car is a lot nicer than Louis or any of his
homies vehicles, so I must have been too injured to skillfully elude. I must
have crashed, and they left me there for dead. That is why I lied to the
investigators about not remembering *anything* because I don't want them
to know I am associated with Louis Conoral. Asshole (my dad) somehow
knows it has something to do with drugs.

Dr. Sherman enters the room. Asshole and Ryan are still here.

"You can go home tomorrow afternoon," Dr. Sherman says. "I want
to give your foot another night before you leave." He smiles at me, and
gently touches my left foot, wrapped in a cast.

I haven't gotten a chance to walk on it yet. When I move my toes, it's sore all the way through. It feels like there's a large bruise covering my entire foot.

"He won't have any trouble walking?" my father asks the doctor.

"Or running?" I ask.

"Aside from soreness, you'll feel off-balance," say Dr. Sherman. "You might need physical therapy."

The doctor continues talking as I space out. My father and Dr. Sherman are having a conversation about something that doesn't interest me. All I hear is "toe," "assault," "recovery," and "physical therapy." I tune in when I hear my father say, "Thanks for everything, Doctor. We'll let you know."

"Thank you," says Ryan.

"Thanks," I say, looking out the window.

I stare out there for what seems to be hours. My father is staring at me. His eyes are pink and his pupils dilated. He doesn't blink.

"Why are you looking at me like that?" I ask without looking at him.

He remains still.

I stare into his unemotional glare. I nibble on my thumb-nail, attempting to distract myself from discomfort, a feeling my father hasn't given me in years.

"How much more trouble do you plan on getting yourself into, Randy?" Asshole says, trying to sound important.

"This is the last of it," I say. "I'm out of trouble." I highly doubt I am though.

"You really disappoint me," he says.

I wonder if I wasn't in this fucking hospital bed, would I take my own father's face off right now? Perhaps kick him in the nuts until they crack?

"I don't need this right now," I say. "All I need is your suppo..."

"I don't understand you," he says, interrupting me.

"I'm not asking for your understanding," I emphasize, trying not to raise my voice. "I'm asking for your support."

The look on his face shows me he couldn't care less.

"Doesn't it concern you that somebody dismembered your son? Doesn't it concern you that two different sets of detectives have come to this room to interview your son while he is recovering from an attack?"

"I'm goin' to the cafeteria," says Ryan, avoiding involvement in an argument. On his way out, he bumps into Dr. Jenkins.

"You must be Ryan. I have heard a lot about you," Dr. Jenkins says, shaking Ryan's hand.

"Who are you?" Ryan asks.

"I am Dwight. I am Randy's doctor," Dr. Jenkins says.

"Well, I'm going to eat. It was nice meeting you."

Ryan leaves.

"You too, Ryan," Dr. Jenkins calls out as Ryan walks away. "Randy, Detective George just told me! What happened?"

Jenkins approaches. He shakes his head softly, upset by my condition. His hand grabs onto mine.

"I'm glad you're okay, Randy."

I overact the bond, trying to make Asshole jealous.

"I don't want to sell drugs anymore, Dr. Jenkins," I say proudly. "I want to start doing the right thing, no matter what the cost."

"Don't sound too proud Randy," my father interrupts. "Lying to investigators isn't a good start at your clean new life."

"You must be Kenneth," Dr. Jenkins smiles.

My father stands and shakes his hand.

"I wasn't aware Randy was in therapy," my father says.

"Oh yes, your son is trying to better himself," Dr. Jenkins says. "He's doing a very good job."

"My brother is also a doctor, and I know how passionate you people are about your jobs," Asshole begins. "But, my son doesn't look like he's in very good condition, now does he?"

"Randy being in a car accident has nothing to do with therapy, sir," Dr. Jenkins says.

"Randy, why don't you tell your doctor how you got in the car crash. Then have him explain why his therapy doesn't seem to be getting you any further away from trouble," my father says to me as he snatches his coat from the chair.

"Randy, did you go over to that man's house to pick up drugs?" Dr. Jenkins asks me.

"No, I mean, I told him I was coming to pick them up, but ultimately my plan was to tell him that I wasn't going to sell drugs anymore," I say.

"You see," Dr. Jenkins tells my father.

"I've heard the story before," Asshole snaps, ready to leave.

"The last thing I want to do, Mr. Mulray, is to make enemies with you," Dr. Jenkins says, holding his aggression back, even though he probably wants to sock my father up too. "Perhaps you would be interested in joining Randy during..."

A red figure walks by. Yeval? I sit and worry as my father and Dr. Jenkins continue arguing. About a minute later, I see the red figure again. It *is* Yeval. I sit up, and turn to hop off the tall hospital bed.

Concerned Yeval has something important to show me and forgetting my left leg has survived a butchering, I stand and put all my weight on my foot. Without delay, there is a pain in my left foot that forces a shout, "ouch!". Then, my left side collapses and I land on my shoulder. More embarrassed than anything, I pretend like it's nothing and attempt to crawl out of the room to find Yeval.

"Nurse," Dr. Jenkins says.

"Randy, come here Son," my father says softly. It's the first time he's talked to me with concern since...I can't even remember when.

Dr. Jenkins grabs my left shoulder and my father grabs my right shoulder. A nurse, a homely elderly nurse, comes running down the hallway to assist.

"Get his feet, nurse," Dr. Jenkins commands.

"I saw something out there," I tell Dr. Jenkins, while they carry me back to the bed.

"We'll take care of it, Randy," my father says, though I highly doubt he has a clue what I'm talking about.

They quickly set me back on the bed. I pull Dr. Jenkins's shoulder to me, and whisper in his ear, "Yeval is out there. Slayer is about to strike again."

"Does he need to be sedated?" my father asks the nurse.

"I appreciate your support, Father and Dr. Jenkins," I say, suddenly calm and relaxed. "But I think I should probably get some sleep."

"I'll stay while you sleep," my father offers.

"No. Go home. Sleep in your own bed. But I appreciate it."

"Are you sure?" he says.

"Yes. Thanks for everything," I say, trying to hurry them out.

"Okay, well, you know to call if you need anything, alright?" my father tells me.

"Alright," I say.

My father walks out with the nurse.

"I think that's the first time my father has ever comforted me," I tell Dr. Jenkins, even though I can remember when I was a kid and my father used to comfort me, a lot. It's probably been the first time since I was seventeen though.

"He seems like a nice man, but I understand why you..." Dr. Jenkins begins.

"You fucker!" I shout at Yeval, who stares at me from the doorway, smiling his stupid smile. At first Dr. Jenkins thinks I'm talking to him, but I point to the doorway and say, "It's Yeval."

Dr. Jenkins looks right at Yeval and Yeval looks right back. "Hello, Dwight," Yeval says to Dr. Jenkins.

"I don't see anything, Randy," Dr. Jenkins says.

"No, of course you don't," I say, leaning my head back against the pillow. "It's all in my head."

Yeval sticks around until Dr. Jenkins takes his leave. He just stands there staring at me, and I find it so distracting that I can't possibly concentrate on anything else. Yeval vanishes when Dr. Jenkins walks out the door. I have an appointment with him next Wednesday.

I don't see Yeval for the rest of that night. But I have a feeling I will see him soon. What did he want? Why didn't he say much?

CHAPTER 19

# Concert

The last two weeks I stayed low key. I went to physical therapy, two Dr. Jenkins appointments, the movie theater five times (all shitty movies), and to Maple Way to hang out with Ryan once. I listened to nothing but The Prodigy's "Fat of the Land" album continuously while driving from destination to destination. The album is a personal favorite ever since its release in 1997. The album was the fastest selling album out of the UK *ever!*

"Fat of the Land" stirred up a bit of controversy at the time of it's release because the music video for Prodigy's first single off that album, *Firestarter*, was deemed "too scary" for children in the UK. The album also featured *Smack My Bitch Up*, a song that totally made feminist groups throw a fit. The song has nothing to do with abusing women. It's just a dance song that only has two lines in it, "Change my pitch up; Smack My Bitch Up," which is *only* a sample taken from Untramagnetic MC's *Give The Drummer Some*, so I don't understand how these feminist bitches can be so naïve. It's like...they didn't even listen to the song.

A personal favorite off that album is the closing track called *Fuel My Fire*, which is a cover of the L7 song. There is a line in the song that I totally think is brilliant, yet simple: "People like you just fuel my fire". That is the perfect phrase to use on somebody who has just pissed you off. I decided to pass that line off as mine, when I started using it last week. I was playing chess at Oliver Stone Park with some guy who never talks. He said, "Checkmate," and I responded, "People like you just fuel my fire." Later that day, I was crossing the street and some *gangsta* chatting on his *mobilephone* in his *ride* wasn't watching the road and he almost hit me. He had the nerve to honk but then realized that I had the right-of-way and waved in apology. Nevertheless, I yelled, "People like you just fuel my fire."

Right now, I'm driving with Morgan to go see Elton John live. I don't have Elton playing in the car, nor have I listened to him at all since I purchased the tickets. I am afraid I'll get burnt out if I listen to him constantly like I usually do. I have high hopes for this show.

I am fed up with Morgan. She's in a fairly good mood today, but I was totally turned off when she farted in the passenger's seat and didn't have the valor to admit she did it. Sure, we just had Mexican, but still it's gross. I know I didn't fart, and she was the only other person in the car. I'm almost about to pull the car over, get out, walk around to the passenger's side, open the passenger door, and pull her out by her hair when she calls Bob Dylan country.

At the moment we are stuck in traffic, and I have "Freewheelin' with Bob Dylan" playing. The stupid bitch says, "I didn't know you liked country, Randy."

It's not fucking country! It's called folk, you stupid skanky cunt!

"It's not country, it's folk, honey," I say.

We get to the venue and our seats are the second shittiest seats in the joint. "How the fuck did this happen when I bought the tickets the minute they were on sale?" I ask myself.

The lights fade, and the wind-sound from the beginning of *Funeral for a Friend/Love Lies Bleeding* (Elton's best song, without a doubt) fades in, and the crowd starts cheering. I scream at the top of my lungs like a little queer pumped to see Elton John in person. A sweet looking teenage girl (I hope I have a daughter who is as cute as her) sits in the row in front of us between her mother and father. She jumps out of her seat excited to see Elton. Some middle-aged trophy-wife sitting next to me screams louder than I've ever heard anyone scream, "Sit down!" in a very mean manner. The teenage girl sits back down, red-faced, and begins to tear up. "That was fucked up," I say not loud enough for anyone to hear. The girl's father turns around and stands up.

"Everybody else is standing!" the father says.

"Sit down!" the trophy wife shouts loudly again, her face red in anger, eyes bulging out of her head.

"Okay, okay," the bitch's husband says softly, trying to keep the peace.

The father remains standing. "Sit down!" the trophy wife screams at him again.

"Shut up!" the father rightfully yells back in her face.

"Sit down!"

"Okay, let's just enjoy the show," the bitch's husband says, holding his wife back as she leans down towards the girl's father.

"You keep her under control," the father says to the bitch's husband, pointing his finger at the bitch.

"Okay, okay," the husband says softly, reaching his hand out toward him, preparing to hold him back from his bitch wife.

"Sit down!"

The father gets up in the bitch's face. "You're a BITCH!" he screams.

"Sit down!"

"Okay, okay," the husband continues saying, nervously tense.

"Bitch!" the father says one last time, and then sits back down. He hugs his daughter and says something to his wife who appears to also be upset.

The bitch's husband is trying very hard not to crack a smile.

"Don't you fucking laugh at me!" the trophy wife yells in her husband's ear and then gets up. She walks past me and Morgan, when I yell in her face, "Sit down!"

"Fuck you," she says and leaves.

The piano solo is about to start. The crowd roars as Elton walks out on stage, takes a bow, and starts his solo on the piano.

I look over at the husband, now sitting alone watching the show. Even in the dark arena I can see in his eyes that he is let down. He lives with that bitch wife of his everyday. I can tell he is miserable. I'm sure he was looking forward to Elton, but she ruined it for him like she probably ruins a lot of things. She didn't just ruin the show for him but for the teenager girl and her family too. Why can't people be polite? How do people get the nerve to talk to complete strangers the way they do? And then it hits me. There are people out there who will make your life a living hell because they aren't getting what they want. The trophy wife ruined the concert for herself and four other people because the excited young girl, who was just happy to see Elton, jump out of her seat in front of her. Then I also realize, this is a reflection of Morgan. It is totally something she would do. And I know that I have to get her out of my life because she has brought nothing to me but trouble. She steals from me, she calls me names, she cheats on me, she smokes the marijuana I try to sell, and she doesn't appreciate the food I put on the table or the roof over her head. It makes me wonder, why is she with me if she thinks I'm just someone to shit on? I am being used. There is no love between us. We are together because we are afraid. She's afraid of being homeless, moneyless, and drugless. I'm afraid of being alone. And at the high point of my year, seeing Elton John live, I feel like shit. During my favorite song I realize that this relationship has meant and taught me nothing.

"The roses in the window box have tilted to one side," Elton sings the first line of the *Love Lies Bleeding* half and I scream in joy like a little queer. "Everything about this house was born to grow and die," I sing along with Elton. It scares me how much I can relate to this song, yet I hadn't noticed it before. "And it doesn't seem a year ago to this very day; you said, 'I'm sorry, honey, don't change the pace, I can't face another day.'"

Elton sings us through some classics and some new songs. The show is very good. Elton is amazing as usual, and the sound quality is magnificent (unlike the disappointing speaker sound of the Gordon Lightfoot show two months earlier). But something catches my eye. In the dark corner of the exit on our side of the balcony, is Yeval, and he is signaling me to come down.

I want to ignore him and enjoy the concert. I don't want to think about death, destruction and all the other pain that Yeval brings me. But I know that I might be able to save someone's life tonight or in the future if I see what Yeval has to offer. So, I slide past Morgan, and down into the lobby where I see Yeval. He walks away, but signals me to follow. So I do.

Elton has just started *Someone Saved My Life Tonight*.

I find the Pearl floating above a trash container near one of the exits on the bottom floor.

I'm in the Dark Room. Yeval waits. I take a seat. The yellow curtain opens. The screen shows a woman sobbing in the dark corner of a closed doorway that says, "EMPLOYEES ONLY".

The woman is curled on the ground in darkness. Light shines on the right side of her face, and music blares loudly. It sounds like Elton John. As I sit in the red chair next to Yeval, I feel like I am so close to her. Then she looks up.

It's the woman who was sitting next to me. She is looking right into the eyes of the Slayer and she doesn't even know it.

"Run," I yell, immediately realizing that I am near her and that I can save her and capture Slayer.

"I'd like to be left alone," she says. "Go away."

I look under my seat to get the ruby to escape. But it isn't there.

"Where's the ruby?" I ask Yeval.

"It's somewhere," Yeval says. "I hide it in a different place every time."

"Help me find it," I tell him.

"No. Watch," he tells me, pointing up to the screen.

I look up at the screen to see a fist pounding into the poor trophy-wife's face. She screams loudly, but nobody can hear her.

I crawl along the black floor, rubbing the palms of my hands along every inch of it.

"Get up," I tell Yeval, who is sitting in his seat, watching the woman being clobbered to death.

I realize that time is of the essence, so I push Yeval out of his seat from behind. Yeval refuses to stand up, so I slip the chair out from under him once two of the chair's legs are off the ground. I run the palms all over the red chair, making sure the ruby hasn't camouflaged with it.

"You bastard!" Yeval yells at me, as he lays on the ground. "How dare you throw me around. I'm in your head!"

As I rub his chair with my palms, the flesh on my palms begins to burn. I look at my palms, juicy with fresh burn-wounds, and then look back at the chair. The chair looks no different.

"I'm in your head, Randy," Yeval says to me. "I can do whatever I want to you! The pain is psychological, and you'll feel it until *I* want it to stop."

Then, in a millisecond, the red chair turns charcoal-black and flashes. Heat blows in my face. My eyes burn and I can't breathe.

"You hideous bastard," I shout, rubbing my sore eyes with burnt palms.

My eyes recover and I search the windowsill. I look out both windows. The unicorns in the right window are running closer, and the woman in the organ spotted dress is skipping through the fields, unfazed by the galloping horses. She is skipping and laughing with a little boy.

The window to the left looks the same. Except now there is a man, an older man, walking down the dry dirt path. It looks like he's gasping for air. He holds his neck and stumbles as he walks. His skin looks bright pink, as if on fire, except there's no flame.

I finally see a twinkle on the curtain left of the screen. The ruby is hanging from the fabric on the yellow curtain. I run over to grab it.

When I grab it in my hand, I see that the Slayer is just finishing slicing off the trophy-wife's ears. Her nose has already been cut in half, and I can literally see the cartilage in the center. Both of her eyes have been popped like zits, their pupils look like little green/yellow bb's, as they drip downward. Her eyeballs have been cut open and hallowed out.

I find myself laying down against the dumpster. One of the guards walks up to me and asks me if I have a ticket. I show it to him, and he leaves me alone. I look down at my palms which still hurt like hell but aren't burnt anymore. I'm freaked out because I realize just how much Yeval is actually fucking with my mind now.

I run all over the large arena looking for the corpse. I search every corner of the two story venue. I search for thirty minutes before I find the body near an emergency exit on the second floor. She's upright, not too bloody, and "SLAYER" is written on the concrete floor right under her lap in blood.

Hoping that the authorities might be able to gather more evidence with a fresher corpse, I decide to call 911 at a payphone on the opposite side of the arena.

"911 emergency," says the dispatcher.

"I have killed another," I say, disguising my voice. "This is the Seattle Slayer at the Legend Arena." I hang up the phone.

I watch the rest of the show from the railing of the second floor, near my actual seat. I can't bear to look at that woman's husband's face knowing what happened to his wife. The concert goes on for another thirty minutes. I meet Morgan by the food stand.

"Where the fuck were you, Randy!" she says, as if she was worried.

"I didn't want to make everybody in our row stand again," I say.

"That bitch didn't come back either."

"Don't call her that," I say, wrapping my arm around her shoulder as we walk out. I kiss her on her head and tell her that I wanted her to enjoy the concert. She said she did.

On the walk out, the crowd slows down to see paramedics wheel a body covered in white sheets. "Slayer this" and "Slayer that" is what I hear all the way to the fucking car. I am about to puke again but I manage to swallow it half way up my throat.

I silently cry myself to sleep. I wonder if the rest of my life is going to be this fucked up. I could've saved her. It's my fault she is dead.

CHAPTER 20

# Dump

It's been two weeks since the murder at Legend Arena. Detectives Lime and Curtis stopped by earlier last week to "check up on me". They claimed to have been sent by Chief to see if I knew anything special about it. Out of fear that I am still a suspect, I decided to lie and say I didn't know shit. I even claimed that I didn't know Elton was in town. Luckily for me, I used a credit-card that I thought Morgan's grandmother lent her, that Morgan just stole from her. So, it's going to be very difficult for anyone to prove I was at the Elton John show besides Morgan. She's been too worried about stealing the card.

Right now, I am sitting at my computer chair working on my novel. I have been doing this for almost two hours. Difficultly arises when I remember the Slayer special about the detective who said that the suspect who lied to them only hindered their investigation. I don't want to hinder the detectives, so I am feeling really bad about lying to detectives Lime and Curtis. However, I am finding it more and more plausible that I could be arrested again.

Morgan walks in and out of *my* bedroom. The first dozen or so times I think she is just looking for attention, but then it becomes apparent to me that she is getting dressed up. She looks at herself in the mirror as she puts on earrings. She is wearing a one-piece black dress, her skirt so short that you can almost see her underwear.

I had a difficult time pumping her drawers full of semen today because her vagina reeked of oiled-tuna. She looks hot now too, with her cleavage hanging so far out of her dress that one of the nipples is about to peek through. I don't think she's showered in a while. I've been out of drugs for almost ten straight days, but I know she's getting her fix elsewhere.

Someone rings and Morgan buzzes them in as if she's expecting them. After two minutes, she says to me, "Honey, someone is here for you."

*Who the hell could it be?* I walk out of my bedroom and into the living room where I find Morgan and Louis, the wannabe drug-lord who cut off my toe, flirting with each other.

Louis looks at me as I limp out of my bedroom straight faced. He takes out a zip-lock bag full of marijuana.

"It's a little more than an ounce," he says to me.

Morgan takes it from him, opens it up, takes a nugget off, and puts it in a bong.

I'm pissed.

Louis is a Mexican, six-foot five, and weighs about 160 pounds. I'm easily stronger than him, but he's got a really good reach, so I don't know if I could take him. But I'm willing to find out.

"I want you selling before Sunday," he says to me.

"Sunday is the Sabbath," I respond.

"You're looking good girl," he says to Morgan, trying to piss off me even more. Morgan giggles as she exhales. Louis looks back over at me and says, "Sorry," pauses, then continues, "about the toe."

"Come into my room," I say. "Let's talk business."

Louis shrugs his shoulders and follows me in my room.

As I lead Louis into my room, I snatch the Walther P99 from under the comforter at the foot of my bed, and slide it under my waistband and cover it with my t-shirt and hoody.

"What do I have to do in order to get out of this business," I say, my back to him as I take a seat in my computer chair. I spin around and face him.

Louis closes the door without me asking him. He wants this to be private.

"I need you right now. You ain't out until I don't need you. You're lucky to be alive," he says, grinding his teeth and widening his eyes, trying to act like he's angry.

I can tell he's not angry. His adrenalin isn't rushing enough for him to go crazy yet.

"I'm not going to be a part of your shit anymore, Louis," I say as calm as I can, preparing to pull my gat out. "You took my toe, so let's call it even."

"No, that was just a warning," he says. "You fuck with me one more time and I'll kill you."

He walks toward me, pulling a Balisong (butterfly-knife). In a split second, he has it opened, ready and wanting to shred me up.

Every inch of the knife is shiny silver. The blade is so sharp, it would dig into your flesh if you even touched it. There is not a single oil-stain on it, telling me he either just got it or he never uses it.

I decide to play it cool as he approaches. I look intently through his eyes, concentrating on not blinking. I want him to know that there is a reason I'm not scared of him. Most gangsters talk while they are threaten. But Louis isn't talking. Therefore, I conclude this is not a threat. He's moving toward killing his first.

I'm sure he's thinking right now of how he'll get away with it, where he'll dump the body, if he'll get respect from his home-dawgs that are also useless to this world, or if he'll regret it.

I let him walk up to me. The bastard actually steps on both my feet so I can't keep my balance. I wonder if he's aware that my foot is still aching. Rage curves through my body. It is when Louis says, "I fucked Morgan last night," that I decide to whip out my gun, and put the barrel right up against his crotch.

"I know," I said. "I hope you enjoyed it while you still had your balls."

"Yes!" I hear a voice say. "Now make him get on his knees."

"Get on your knees," I tell Louis.

"Fuck you," Louis says, almost scared.

"Yes!" says the voice. It's Yeval, of course. He creeps up on Louis like a lobster from across the room. "Shoot him in the nuts," he tells me.

"Do it, Louis. Stab me. I'm fucking serious," I warn. "You fucked with the wrong white boy."

"Shoot him!" Yeval tells me. "Right in the nuts!"

I fire. But not in his nuts. I fire a warning shot right between his legs. I don't give a shit about the neighbors or cops right now.

Louis jumps, startled.

"On your knees, fuck," I tell Louis.

He obeys.

"Drop the knife," I tell him.

He sets it on the ground next to my left foot. I kick the knife across the room with the side of my foot and violently grab a fistful of Louis's hair. I shove the barrel into his mouth, chipping a few of his teeth. I imagine how fast his heart is racing right now and wonder if my heart was racing this fast when he and his homies cut my toe off.

"You think you'd get away with torturing me and fucking my bitch?" I say violently, feeling like a gangster.

"Shoot him, Randy!" Yeval cheers.

Louis is breathing hard out his nose. He stretches his lips so he can get air through his mouth too, but I just shoved the gat deeper into his throat, so deep that his eyes start tearing.

"If you choke, your head gets blown off," Yeval says. "Tell him that, Randy."

"If you choke, your head gets blown off," I look into Louis's eyes, promising him. "I will do it too."

Louis closes his eyes, concentrating on not choking. I am tempted to shove the barrel even deeper into his throat so I can kill him. But, Morgan walks in and ruins everything.

"Oh my god!" she says. "Randy, stop that!"

She starts crying.

I cock the gun and start thrusting the gun back and forth in Louis's mouth.

"This is what it must have felt like, while your dick was in her mouth," I say to Louis.

He is stunned, but still not in shock. The idea that the gun could accidentally go off right now makes me want to pull the trigger even more. It would be perfect for his brains to spatter all over Morgan's pretty slutty face. This is the first time in my life I ever wanted to kill someone.

"Yeah, suck that cock," I say, moving the gun back and forth. "You're not sucking, dipshit!" I yell aggressively.

Morgan drops to her knees, screaming, pleading. "Randy, please."

"Yes! Yes!" Yeval says excitedly, clapping his hands and jumping up and down. "Now, do it. Do the deed."

Rage pulses through me like I have never felt before. I actually enjoy being this mad. I feel like God. I am literally holding life in my hands.

I swallow and put pressure on the trigger.

"If I wanted to, I could end it."

As my finger pressures the trigger, as I prepare myself to finally do what Yeval wants, and as I feel the indescribable rush of life in my hands, I notice something. Morgan is crying. Morgan never cries...except when she doesn't get her way.

"Why are you crying?" I ask confused, taking the gun out of Louis's mouth.

She just sits there, almost in shock. I notice she's sweating.

"Why are you crying!?" I yell. "Over this useless fuck!" I point to Louis with my gun. I stare him straight in the eye, pointing the gun at his head, just to watch Morgan cry some more. "You think this fuck cares about you, Morgan? You think he'll treat you like a person? You think he'll take care of you like I did? Do you think anything you do for him will be appreciated? No, Morgan! No!" I am screaming at this point. My throat begins to get scratchy. "But, you still shed a tear for him," I say, softening my voice. "Yet, I took great care of you and you never cried for me. You never thanked me. You never cared about me. Just my luck, I should have figured." I take my gun away from Louis's head.

"You see," I begin to lecture both of them. "This is why I'm uptight. Because when I am a nice guy, I am a push over. Louis, I treated you with respect, like every employee should their boss. But you treated me like shit, you ripped me off, you wouldn't let me quit, and you *fucked* my girlfriend. Morgan, I cared for you more than anybody will ever care for your useless ass. You have never done anything with your life and you have nothing to offer. Yet, you still got the chance to have yourself a boyfriend who you continuously fucked over." I put the loaded gun back against Louis's head. "So typical. You both deserve to die."

I can literally see Louis's brown skin turn red. Morgan is twitching at this point.

"Then kill them," Yeval says.

"Shut up, Yeval," I say, not caring that I am the only one who knows he's there.

I take the gun away from his head again.

"I want you both out of here right now. Morgan, you just go. Fuck your shit, all of it was stuff I bought you anyway. You leave right now. You too, Louis."

Louis slowly crawls backward. He stands up, Morgan helping him. They both stare at me as they back out of the room.

"I see either of you again, I'll kill you both."

They back all the way out and I hear the front door slam shut. I stand there for an hour, just thinking.

What did Yeval do to me?

Am I dangerous? Was I enjoying it or was it in the heat of the moment?

Yeval talks to me, but I don't hear him. As I stand there with the gun still in my hand, I wonder if I should just put the barrel in my mouth and paint my bedroom with my own blood. I convince myself I should but am too numb to lift the gun.

I call Dr. Jenkins's emergency number (I think it's his cell), but he doesn't pick up.

I cry. I lay on the hardwood floor in my bedroom and think about how pathetic I am. I think about how much I have screwed my life up. I think about the others who screwed up my life.

I think about how people easily remember bad things, but easily forget the good things. Knowing this, is it worth it to be good—taking into consideration that people are more likely to forget about it? What is the point of being a good person? I've tried and it never worked for me. But being a bad person gets you what you want faster. You don't earn what you want, you just take it.

Why should I be a good person? It has never done me any good.

CHAPTER 21

# Motel

Chief Milton, Lime, and Curtis decide to take me on a little field trip to one of the crime scenes. It's where they first found me. You know, that whore (Tracey I think her name was) that got a hose shoved in her vagina.

"Gamma-Hydroxybutyric acids were found during the autopsy," says Chief.

"The date rape drug," Curtis adds.

"But there was no semen, no condom, no evidence of any sexual activity," Chief Milton continues.

"He drugged her so he could tie her up," I say.

"That's what we figured," Lime agrees.

"It's obvious," that fat-bastard Curtis says.

It is just us four in the hotel room. The room is clean, but I manage to spot some blood stains on the wood floor. The bed has been replaced with a new one, but that doesn't make the setting any less haunting. I wonder how many people have slept in this room since Tracey was killed.

"A witness, the manager, said that he saw a man, the same man who checked into the room, leave the motel less than an hour after he checked in," Chief Milton tells me.

"That fits his profile," I say.

"I don't know," says Lime. "Most serial killers linger in the aftermath as long as possible, unless it's public. Here, the Slayer had the privacy to enjoy what he had done."

"The Slayer isn't like other serial killers," says Detective Curtis.

"Yep," I agree. "That's how the Slayer works. In and out as fast as possible. That's why he never gets caught. He doesn't enjoy the mayhem as much as he enjoys the reaction. It's the media building him up that gets the sick bastard off."

We hang out in silence for a few seconds, lost in thought.

"Yep," I say. "He just wants to see the blood, and watch his victim's last breath."

"How did she die, Randy?" Curtis asks.

I try to think. I can't remember. Did I see her die? Come on Randy, think! No. I didn't. This was when I found the ruby in the Dark Room, and escaped. Then I drove to the motel. Now I remember.

"I didn't see how she died," I say. "I found a ruby looking thingy in the Dark Room that lets me out. Yeval hides it in a different place every time I go in there, so he can enjoy forcing me to watch the murders through Slayer's eyes."

I don't even realize that these guys have no idea what I'm talking about.

"You see, he's just a nutcase," Curtis says to Chief.

"So," I say. "You just asked a question you already knew the answer to, just for the sake of making me looking stupid and crazy. Is that it?"

"Yeah," Curtis says, knowing he has succeeded.

"You're a cocksucker," I tell him.

"What! What do you know about anything, you little faggot?" The fat bastard runs up in my face, pushing his forehead against mine, and stares me deeply in the eyes.

"Hey, maybe it's you, you bastard," I say. "Yeah. I know what I did and didn't see, so I know that I am right. Maybe you're saying I'm full of shit because it's your eyes I'm seeing through."

"Enough," says Chief, coming between us.

Lime softly pulls me away as I take my turn drilling my forehead into Curtis's.

"You'll have to kill me in order to shut me up," I say, when I'm pulled away.

"I'll get enough evidence to prove you're a part of this, you little shit," says Curtis.

Things cool down and Lime walks me outside. We walk through the parking lot.

"We didn't get much solved today," he says to me, putting sunglasses on.

"What do you think happened?" I ask.

"I think she was lured into the motel, drugged, and tortured to death. Nothing you can't tell me."

"I'm sorry if I don't have anything insightful for you, but would some-one who's full of shit know that her eyes and mouth were sewn shut. That she was cut open while she was still alive?"

"But," he says.

"But the newspapers didn't say shit about any of that. I know," I say. "So either I killed her, or I am telling the truth."

"How do I know you didn't kill her?"

"You guys have been having a pretty difficult time charging me, haven't you? No evidence on me. I'm confident you'll never link any evidence to me because I never did anything."

"Yeah?" Lime says, not knowing what else to say.

"Yeah. You can either suspect me, or you can believe me and make the most of my help."

He takes out a cigarette from a shiny silver case. Before putting it back in his pocket, he hold it out offering me one. I haven't smoked in almost eight years, but I decide to take it. He lights it for me and lights his own.

"I can tell the Chief believes me," I say.

"I think he does too. But, the Chief has a weird imagination. Too weird. Perhaps he wants a psychic detective to make things interesting. Maybe he even wants this whole thing to get bigger. How can it get bigger."

"Wait. What's so weird about Chief?"

"Almost thirty years on the case and it hasn't been solved. His unit has solved every murder he's been assigned to, except this one."

"Well, Slayer is smart," I say, defending the Chief.

"Forget it," he says.

"Why?"

"Just forget it."

There is an uncomfortable silence.

Lime takes a drag of his cigarette and says, "So, tell me everything you know."

CHAPTER 22

# Dinner

I am eating bacon chowder with garlic bread. This is the first time I've eaten on the dinner menu at Hermit Lounge. Both my father and Ryan are eating a Thai dish (Phad Thai, I think), saying how much it sucks.

My father has called me three times this week. He usually calls me three times a year. I suppose after my assault, he has been worried about me. Good. He should.

The two of us have seen each other ten times in the last two weeks. It seems like we are becoming father and son again. Two months ago I would've puked at the thought of me liking my dad. But now, it feels good to have a father-figure again. I haven't felt that in a long time.

I brought Caroline with us, just to show my father that I am getting my life back together. He always liked Caroline. She is having the dinner salad.

We chat about bullshit and laugh loudly, like the fortunate rich white people we are. We order another bottle of red wine—Moscato d'Asti. Life seems simple. My father and I are starting to see eye to eye, I'm back with the girl I've dreamed about and am out of the drug business. But I am not comfortable.

I can't come to terms with my brother's retardation. I did this to him.

I still can't come to terms with my mother's death. I killed her.

I look around the table and see everyone laughing. I laugh too even though I don't hear the joke. And though I'm bathing in the bliss I dreamed of for so many years, I worry that this won't always last. There are too many unanswered questions before I can be at ease.

I hear the high-pitch sound of the triangle and I know it's Yeval. I turn to the bathroom, where I see him peeking at me.

"Excuse me a moment," I say to my family as I get up to go to the bathroom.

"What do you want," I ask Yeval, locking myself inside the bathroom stall for privacy. "I don't see the Pearl. Where is it?"

"I am here just to talk," he says.

"Well, I don't want to talk to you," I say. "You bring me nothing but pain. If you got something useful for me, then *show* me. You *talking* is something I've listened to for too long. Years!"

I unlock the stall.

"Oh, but you're gonna want to hear this," he says, smiling happily.

"What is it?"

"Get cozy," he tells me. I lock the stall again and sit on top of the toilet. "It's been a while."

"Almost two weeks, Yeval. I'm not talking to you unless you got something useful for me."

"You're in luck," he says enthusiastically. "I am here to help you. You have everything to solve who the killer is, but you can't do it. So, that's why I'm here."

"Yeah?" I ask, eager for Yeval to continue. "You're going to help me find the killer?"

"The killer will strike soon. It will be someone you know. Someone you care about."

"What! Wait! Someone I know! Tell me what to do!" I beg Yeval for the first time in my life. After all the pain Yeval has put me through, I never would have imagined that I'd beg him for something.

"Why should I tell you? You're so close to solving it."

"I am? How? Wait," I say, realizing. "You're a figment of my imagination. If you know something, then I must know it."

"Figment of your imagination? Well," Yeval breaks sentence in laughter. He is actually cracking up, something I have never seen him do before. "It's funny you say that.

"Let me ask you something," he continues. "Why do you fucking act like you owe the world something?"

"Because I offered nothing else to it. Because my mother tried to save me and I killed her. Because my brother is retarded thanks to me. I am a lost cause," I say this quickly, eager to confess.

"Interesting," he says, walking back and forth in the small bathroom stall. "Now answer me this. Why is what you see in the Dark Room accurate to the actual killings?"

"Uh, because I can see through the killer's eyes," I say, unsure.

"True," he says. "What else?"

"Uh, because you're in the killer's mind as well as mine?"

"True, go on," Yeval says, holding back a laugh.

Yeval is looking at me and laughing at me. It's as if I've figured something out and I don't know it. Then it comes to me. Something so obvious. "If Slayer and I both see you," I say. "Then, you must be in both our minds."

"Why do you sound unsure? It's obvious."

I swallow. My throat is sore. I am afraid of the question I'm about to ask and terrified of the answer. "Are we one mind, Yeval?"

Yeval doesn't answer. He just laughs.

"Answer me! Am I Slayer! Is me going into the Dark Room a way of you taking over my body?" And that's it. I have it figured out. I realize that I am the Slayer.

Sweat drips down my forehead. I don't know what to do. I can't stop gasping for air.

To myself, I think that if I were to ever do anything for the world, it would be to stop the Slayer. In order to do this, I have to stop me. There's no two ways about it, I have to be stopped.

I unlock the stall and walk out.

"Where are you going?" Yeval calls.

I can't kill myself. That wouldn't bring justice to those I have hurt. I must turn myself in and rot to death in a cell.

I peek out the bathroom door and look at my family. I look at my father who is going to be more disappointed in me than he has ever been before. Then to my brother who laughs happily, and I think to myself that if it wasn't for me, he would've been normal. Then I see Caroline. My Caroline. The only person who understands me. The only person who loved me back as much as I loved her. The only person I wanted to spend every moment of my life with.

I want to die. I deserve to die. I was never meant to be. All I have done is cause people pain. And I must be stopped before I can hurt anymore.

Without a second thought, I sprint out of the bathroom and out of the café. I don't go unnoticed. I knock a waiter carrying a dish over, breaking it. I think I even hear my father yell my name, concerned.

I run out, not looking back. I run and run faster than I've ever ran before. I run to the police station.

CHAPTER 23

# Confession

I jam my wrist against the front door of the police station trying to push it inward. The sign says "PULL".

I ask the officer at the booth to buzz me in immediately so I can catch Detective Lime before he goes home for the day. The officer tells me that Lime can't come out at the moment but that I can wait on the bench.

"Fuck your mother," I say out of breath.

I attempt to push open the secured door that leads to the station itself, but even someone as tough as me can't force it open.

While I'm kicking and screaming like a child, the officer gets backup. Three more officers come out, and I shout to them, "Stay back! I'm the Seattle Slayer."

They pause, look at each other, then look back at me.

Then...they burst into laughter.

"Sure kid," says one officer.

"Did you kill your first victim when you were an infant?" says another.

"The Seattle Slayer has been at large for almost thirty years," says the one who was at the booth.

"How old are you?" asks the fourth officer.

"Twenty-nine," I say, embarrassed of my age for the first time in my life.

"Yeah, exactly," says the one who was at the booth. "Check yourself into an asylum, not a police station. I got work to do."

"What's going on?" asks Chief Milton, who just walked in.

"Chief!" I exclaim in relief.

"Mulray," he says to me. "You don't look so good, kid."

"I'm him."

Chief tilts his head, wondering if I'm talking about what he thinks I'm talking about.

"I'm the Seattle Slayer."

Hours later, I'm sitting in the interrogation room, sipping on some coffee that Detective Lime brought me. Next to me sits the fat ass lawyer the court appointed to me the first time I was arrested. Hopefully, now that I'm on good terms with my father, he can get me a better lawyer (or at least one I like). What am I saying? My dad will hate me more than he's ever hated me when he finds out about this.

"Everything you say is true, Randy," says my fat ass lawyer, "then why don't you just plead guilty by insanity? You're obviously an unstable person. They'll throw out the death penalty at least."

"I'm guilty, so I'm pleading guilty."

"But the death penalty..."

"I deserve to die," I interrupt him, about to tell him to take a hike, but I'm interrupted by Detectives Lime and Curtis. Lime smiles politely at me, but kind of has an mortified look on his face. Curtis looks like he's trying not to smile. Chief Milton walks in after and sits down across from me.

"Randy," Chief says, exasperated. "What's going on?"

"I confessed to the killings by the 'Notorious Seattle Slayer'. What are you so confused about?"

"What, kiddo," shouts George Curtis. "Did mommy and daddy not give you enough attention when you were a kid?"

"My mom's dead, Fat," I reply with the quickness.

"Are you on drugs?" asks the Chief, putting on glasses.

I didn't know the Chief wore glasses.

"No," I say. "Why aren't we talking about the crimes I committed?"

"Well, Randy," Chief Milton begins, looking back at the two detectives who obviously know the answer. "We ruled you out a while ago."

"What?" I say.

"We have fingerprints of the Seattle Slayer," Chief says, sipping out of his mug. "We tried to match your fingerprints when we first arrested you, but the tests came back negative. No DNA match either." He pauses and takes a deep breath.

He feels sorry for me. They all do. Even my lawyer. I am pathetic.

"We ruled you out as a suspect, Randy," says Lime. "So why are you doing this? Do you know something we don't?"

"I have told you everything," I shout defensively.

I feel my face blush. I'm overheated. My mouth is dry. I can't blink.

Yeval stands in the corner opposite Lime and Curtis and laughs, "Fraud! You're a fraud!"

"Everything I've seen in my visions..." I say

I pause.

"Yes," says Curtis in a condescending tone.

"Was true," I continue. "I saw it all. It all really happened."

I throw my head in my hands and go silent.

"What do you think, Chief?" asks Curtis. "Do you think he knows anything?"

"No," Chief responds quickly. "He's a nut who belongs in the nuthouse. He's a waste of our time. Let's go."

Chief stands up, and walks out the door.

"You're not being charged with anything, Randy," he says as he exits. "Go home."

Curtis follows Chief out.

I stand out in the hall, after my lawyer leaves, when Lime approaches me and says, "You're insane, Randy." The look on his face is daunting. He's angry with me.

"Yeval convinced me that I did it."

"You're a nut, just like the Chief said."

I put my head down, avoiding eye contact. I feel like a disobedient dog.

"But I believe you," he adds.

I look up in relief.

"You do!"

"Yes." He leans forward and whispers in my ear. "I found a match on those fingerprints."

"Well, why don't you do something," I shout.

Lime tells me to shh.

"You can stop another death from occurring."

"It's not that easy," he says.

"Why! Why is it so difficult to arrest the killer," I say in anger.

"I'll give you a ride," he says, tugging at me to follow.

I pull away and say, "Why?"

"Come on."

"No! Tell me why."

"I'll tell you in the car."

"No, you tell me now, you stupid bastard," I say, grinding my teeth, about to explode. "Tell me now."

He whispers, "Because the fingerprints match Detective Curtis's."

CHAPTER 24

# Ride

Lime drives a dark-silver 2005 Trailblazer. When I slide into the pas-senger seat and feel the brand new leather seat, I immediately forget about the Slayer issue and become jealous.

"I should get me one of these," I say.

"Forget about the fucking car, Randy," Lime says, as he gets in. He's right. I have more important things to worry about. "Now listen…"

He starts the car.

"You can't say anything."

He pulls out of the lot.

"Why not?"

"There's a reason I'm keeping this a secret," he explains. "First; Curtis might not even have done it. He may just been careless at a crime scene. Second; I wasn't supposed to run the fingerprint test on him. I could lose my job if…"

"Fuck your job, Lime. You matched someone's fingerprints with the notorious Seattle Slayer. Everyone will honor you."

"Still, you can't tell anyone," he stresses.

"Why!?"

"Because he might not be the Seattle Slayer and I could lose my job. Okay."

"But you found the prints at the crime scene," I say, irritated at how cautious Lime is being. "You found a match."

"They have found other prints at the scenes also, Randy."

"Oh," I say, surprised but disappointed.

"This is just trouble," he says. "Forget I said anything about it."

There is a long silence.

"Ya know," he begins, "when you were arrested, we thought you were actually a copycat—we knew you weren't Slayer."

Someone cuts in front of the car, and Lime honks.

"That prostitute murdered at the motel," he continues, "was the first time Slayer altered his profile."

"Huh?"

"He didn't use a murder weapon originally from the crime-scene."

"Oh yeah. That's right. He brought in a black bag. I totally overlooked that! But what does that prove?"

"Well, we released you after we checked your prints and came up with no match. But you were still a prime suspect of *just* the prostitute murder until the DNA tests came back negative a few days later."

"So you think there's more than one person involved?" I ask.

"That's why I really thought it was you. Your age didn't mean shit. You didn't have to be born when these murders started in order for you to impersonate them now."

"So how am I ruled out as a suspect?" I ask.

"Because your prints matched neither prints obtained recently or decades ago. You and Tracey's DNA didn't the strand of hair found at the crime-scene."

"How do you know it's not hair from a guest that stayed there earlier?"

"Would it be found in the opening of her wounds? Impossible."

I am speechless.

We sit in silence for minutes.

When we are about a mile to my apartment, Lime asks, "So, you said your mom died."

"Yeah. When I was just a little kid. Ten."

"I'm sorry," he says. "I lost my father in a car accident when I was eighteen."

"Yeah, losing a loved one sucks."

"Uh-huh. But isn't it crazy how life just keeps going? Even when you want it to stop and wait for you to get better, it just keeps going. You have to roll with the punches."

He waits for me to respond.

I don't.

"Isn't that right," he says.

"For you, maybe," I say.

"What? What makes your mother's death so different from my father's? Everybody loses a loved one. We have to move on. That's what my father wanted for me. I'm sure that's what your mother wants for you."

"You didn't know my mother, so don't talk about her," I say defensively.

There is an awkward silence.

Traffic stops suddenly. We sit in the jam for several minutes without slipping a sound.

After a few minutes of silence I feel strange. I feel as though Lime has some power over me. Maybe it's something as simple as me feeling his pain. Or maybe it's something more. Whatever it is, I feel comfortable enough to say to him, "I killed her."

"Who?" he says, surprised. "Your mother?"

"Yeah," I say. I look over at him.

He takes his eyes off the road to glance at me. He's not angry. He's not disappointed. He's just...interested.

For the first time since I talked to Dr. Baker, I feel okay opening up and telling my story.

"We were at Alki Beach," I say. "It was 1986. August third, Ryan's birthday. My mother was pregnant with him. My mother and I would go to the beach every sunny day. I remember playing on the sand while she read magazines against a log, sitting on her a purple blanket. We'd have peanut butter and jelly sandwiches, with chunky peanut butter and strawberry seeded jelly on white bread. We'd share a milk that we'd pick up from the market on the way there.

"One day, as I was eating my sandwich, I saw a golden retriever. Two kids were throwing a stick into the water, and the dog would fetch it. Dale was the dog's name, I still remember. I always wanted a golden retriever.

"Anyway, I ran into the water to play with the dog. One of the volleyball players made an enormous kill shot or something, because I remember as the boy threw that stick, he immediately turned around to look at the cheering coming from the volleyball area.

"The kid, who was only half watching, threw the stick over my head. The dog instinctively jump over me, knocking into the water. Next thing I knew, I was sucked out by the tide.

"'Help! Help!' I yelled. I was gasping for air, my face going over and under the water with the waves. To this day, I still don't know if it was just my imagination or if it was for real, but I remember my mother screaming, 'Save my baby!'

"After a minute or two, my head was below the surface. I was breathing in nothing but water. I remember it began to hurt, and I was too scared to think. Next thing I knew, a lifeguard lifted me out, and swam me back to shore.

"When I got there, I found my mother on the ground. Half the beach was crowded around her, while the other half crowded me. I heard the ambulance sirens approach as soon as I was being dragged out of the water. I must have stuck in there for a good three or four minutes."

"You were a tough bastard, even when you were ten," Lime says.

Traffic moves forward.

"I remember sitting up and being scared," I continue. "The people around me were telling me to relax, lay down, breath slowly. But I was scared, Lime. Very scared. More scared than I've ever been. So, I jumped up and ran. Ran to where the other crowd was surrounding my mother. And there, I saw her."

"What did you see?"

"She was holding her stomach, and blood was dripping down her polka-dotted orange dress and down her thighs. I remember saying, 'Mommy?' because I had never seen her cry before. She looked up at me and said to the lifeguard, 'You saved my baby.' Then she looked at one of the paramedics and said, 'Save my other baby, no matter what.' Then, they lifted her in the stretcher, and drove off. They put me in a stretcher too and drove me to the same hospital.

"At the hospital, I got better. At the hospital, Ryan was born. At the hospital, my mother died."

I look up and see Lime looking at the road, though I can tell he has been listening. I notice now that Lime must have looped the block a few times so I could finish my story.

"How'd she die?"

"When I was getting sucked out in the water, my mother jumped up and ran. She tripped in the sand and landed face down right on her stomach."

"Shit."

"She died of internal bleeding. Ryan had permanent brain damage and was born three months premature. They said he weighed 17 ounces."

Silence fills the car. My story has wiped the life out of Lime like it has wiped the life out of me and my father. What kind of life is this?

Lime pulls up to the curb. He pulls out his business card. "Randy, I want you to call me the next time you're in the Dark Room."

"I will," I say, taking the business card.

He puts his hand out and I shake it.

"This is also against the rules, so don't say anything to anybody," he tells me as I get out.

"I won't. It's just between us."

"Good. Well, take it easy," he says.

"I'm sure I'll be talking to you soon."

"Well, let's hope not," he says. "The next time I talk to you will probably be when the Seattle Slayer kills again."

"You're right. I'll try my best not to call you," I say jokingly.

Lime laughs and waves.

I nod my head, close the passenger door, and walk back to my apartment.

I have to call and apologize to my father, Caroline and Ryan for running out on them. I feel better, though. I have one of the detectives' trust. And even though I still feel guilty for my mother's death and Ryan's condition, I feel at ease after opening up to Lime. My burden has been lightened and I have Lime to thank for it. Now, knowing that I'm not the Seattle Slayer, I know what I must do. I must catch him myself. I am Seattle's last hope for survival against the predator who preys on anyone.

So this is how it feels to be altruistic.

I'm going to be the hero.

CHAPTER 25

# Louis

I toss my keys on the counter, throw my hoody on the rocking chair, and jump onto the couch where I quickly fall asleep.

I hear a creaking sound but ignore it. Shortly after, I hear it again.

I doze off and on for about twenty five minutes or so while *Jeopardy!* is muted on the television. As I drift off I become horny. I massage my boner softly through my jeans, pretending it was one of the contestants turning herself on by gripping my crotch.

I hear a creak again. I open my eyes and see Louis looking down at me. His fist hammers into my face and I black out. I wake tied to my rocking chair, soaked in gasoline. Morgan, Louis and Roberto (Louis's handyman) are eating the food from my kitchen. I sit and watch as they tear apart my house.

"They're going to burn you alive," says Yeval, popping out from behind me. "It's going to hurt."

I don't say anything. I just watch. I watch Morgan stuff her face with the pastries I bought at the store earlier this week, and I think to myself how fun it would be to burn her alive. How dare she do this to me. Ah hell. I should've known better all along.

Yeval disappears.

Louis approaches me. He kicks me in the chest, and I rock back and forth in the chair. Louis kicks like a pussy.

"You kick like a pussy, Louis," I say, feeling the knot in my right cheek from when he punched me out.

I can't see the clock or window. I have no idea what time it is. I can't tell if it's day or night.

"Where's the money, shithead?" Louis says to me.

"What money?"

"You know what I'm talking about, cocksucker," he says, then kicks me in the chest again, this time rocking the chair so hard that the chair falls back. I try to push my head forward so as not to hit it on the floor when the chair falls. But my head whips back when the chair hit's the ground, and smashes right into the wooden floorboard.

Louis starts kicking me in the face as I lay helplessly in the rocking chair

"Where's the money, fucker?" is what he is mostly screaming as his eyes go redder with rage and spits flies from his mouth.

One of my molars gets chipped, and my left front tooth gets knocked out during the process. It's kind of strange how sensitive the nerves in your mouth are compared to other parts of your body, because I don't remember feeling this much pain while getting my toe chopped off. I don't remember the last time I felt such agonizing pain, to the point where I start tearing up and screaming.

I am about cry out pitifully for him to stop kicking me, but he stops on his own. I am relieved by the fact that I didn't have to beg this douche-bag for sympathy.

I spit out blood. Lots of it. Despite the blood being thick, it drips from my mouth in large quantities; I spit it on the floor as you'd spit mouth-wash into a sink. The pool of blood lays right by my face, a tooth sliding slowly in the puddle.

Morgan looks at me. I see tears in her eyes. She's probably thinking, *what did they do to his pretty face.*

"I'm not going to ask you again," says Louis, signaling Roberto.

Roberto kneels down beside me, the knife pointed at my heart.

"Roberto will stab you right in the heart if you don't tell us where my money is."

"Goddamnit, Randy, just tell them where the money is," Morgan says, begging me to cooperate.

"This is all your fault, Morgan," I tell her and then look at Louis. "You're going to kill me anyway. I made you my bitch, and the only way for you to live with it is to kill me. You're a coward."

Louis signals Roberto to back off. Robert puts the knife down, but remains kneeling.

"What is it with you, Mulray?" Louis says, kneeling down next to Roberto. "Too much pride to save yourself?"

"There is no fucking money, Louis," I say. "I have no drugs to sell and I don't have a job. I don't make *any* fucking money."

"Well, you should've come up with something, because now you're gonna die," he smiles at me and lights his Zippo. "I can't afford to have you around. You'll just rat me out to the cops."

"Oh my God," I hear Morgan say.

"It's the life we both chose, Louis," I tell him, preparing myself to burn. "We'll always look over our shoulders and we deserve it. But you deserve to be in my position. Killer." Then I spit blood in his face.

"Oh my God," I hear Morgan say again, this time she's screaming it at the top of her lungs. "You said you were just going to hurt him."

"Shut up, bitch," Louis yells at her. "I want to enjoy this."

"Oh my God!" Morgan screams one more time, even louder and with fright not mercy.

I look at Morgan and notice that the bitch isn't even looking at us. She is looking behind us and is terrified. I soon see a man dressed in all black, his face soaked in white paint, standing behind Louis and Roberto. It is Slayer.

"Oh my God," I say.

"Put the lighter out," says Slayer, holding the gun against Louis's head.

Louis shuts the Zippo and looks around. His eyes widen. The look of Louis shocked is almost funny even in a situation as this.

The Slayer instructs all three of them to go into the living room. I lay on the ground trying to remember how to breathe. I have literally shit my pants and I think Louis might have broken my ribs while he was kicking me.

Slayer returns. I look up at him, right into his eyes. The whites of his eyes are rosy. I can't tell if they just look that way because of how white the paint is in comparison, or if the toxin of the paint got into his eyes. I am in such shock, I'm unsure about whether or not I know who the man is.

"Hello, Randy," he says.

*That doesn't look like Detective Curtis.*

As he lifts the rocking chair up, I try to look for characteristics I might remember. There is no facial hair. Of all the unique features that every individual has on their face, Slayer's have been distorted by the pure white paint. All I can see is a nose (I can't tell how big), eyes (brown), thick head of hair (also drenched in white paint), ears (I can't tell how big either) and a mouth.

Slayer pushes the rocking chair, with me still tied to it, into the living room. There, Morgan, Roberto and Louis are all tied individually around their arms and legs, and their mouths are duct-taped shut.

Slayer's bag sits on the coffee-table. With the gun in his left hand, Slayer unzips the bag and digs through it with his right. He takes out a Benchmade Griptilian Knife. Slayer pulls the blade from the rubber handle and holds the silver shiny blade that's at least eight and a half inches long, right up to Louis's face. Louis, sitting between Morgan and Roberto, breaths deeply as Slayer merrily taunts him by waving the blade less than a inch from his nose.

*Wait! Slayer is using a weapon he brought. That doesn't match his profile...but it does match the way Tracey died.*

Slayer cuts the rope Louis is tied up with, freeing him. He rests his right hand on his waist, and raises his left, pointing the gun right at Louis's face.

"Take it," Slayer says, instructing Louis to take the knife.

Louis swallows nervously, sweat dripping from his forehead, and takes the knife.

"Pull down his pants," instructs Slayer.

My heart thumps even harder and faster than it did before. I hope I have a heart attack. I don't look at Morgan crying, or Louis contemplating whether to test Slayer's order. I stare at Slayer's face trying to identify him. What becomes more and more terrifying as time goes on is the certainty that I know him. I recognize the silhouette somehow.

"Do you want to die?" Slayer asks Louis, who hasn't pulled down Roberto's pants.

"Do as I ask, or I will shoot you in the face." Slayer presses the barrel roughly against Louis's jaw. "Don't you know who I am?" Slayer inquires loudly, with passion. This is obviously a high for him.

Louis mumbles something and looks into Slayer's eyes in terror. For the first time, I feel sorry for Louis. He looks genuinely scared.

"What? I didn't hear you," says Slayer.

"You're the Slayer," Louis replies respectfully.

"So, you know what I'll do if you don't listen to me. Now pull down his pants."

What am I doing! Why can't I identify this fucker? It's not like he's wearing a fucking mask. I'm an idiot! I'm a loser! I deserve to die.

"Kill me," I say. "I deserve this."

"Shut the fuck up, Randy," says Slayer.

How does he know my name?

I *really* do deserve to die. He knows me. I must know him.

"You deserve to die, Randy," I hear a voice say, from behind me. Though I can't turn around to see who it is, I know it's Yeval.

"Not now, Yeval," says Slayer.

Yeval walks in front of me, staring at me while I stare at Slayer. Every so often, Slayer glances at Yeval. Slayer can see Yeval.

"Pull down his pants."

Louis swallows. He looks over at his friend tied up helplessly next to him and staring back at him. Louis unbuttons and unzips Roberto's pants, then pulls them down, revealing poker-card boxers. My boxers. Roberto must have stolen them from my drawer before they attacked me.

"The boxers too," commands Slayer.

Louis obeys. He slides down his friend's boxers. Roberto and Louis both stare at Slayer. Roberto stares in anger, while I think that Louis just stares at Slayer to avoid looking at Roberto's penis.

Roberto's pubic-region is covered with dark untrimmed hair. The skin is much paler than the rest of his body, and his penis is obviously much smaller than mine.

"Now suck it," Slayer orders Louis.

"No," Yeval objects.

"What?" asks Slayer.

"Give him the knife," Yeval points at Louis.

"Him?" asks Slayer.

Louis and Roberto are completely confused as Slayer converses with Yeval.

Though tied up, Morgan is able to curl herself into the fetal position. She breaths deeply as tears drip from her closed eyes.

"Make him cut off the other one's penis," says Yeval.

"Cut off his dick," Slayer says to Louis, giving him the knife.

Roberto's eyes widen as Slayer hands the knife to Louis. He looks over at his friend, scared and helpless, as his buddy takes the knife.

"If you point that blade at me, I'll blow your head off," Slayer says. "If you don't cut that dick off, I'll blow your head off. Now do it."

Louis sits there bravely, holding the knife, contemplating whether or not to listen to the evil man holding his life in his hands. Thirty seconds go by and Louis does nothing. Suddenly, Slayer fires a bullet into Louis's knee cap. Chips of bone fly from it, and Louis cries immediately.

"Do it, or the next one is his head," screams Slayer.

Still screaming in unbearable pain, Louis grabs his friend's cock with his right hand. Roberto tries to scream through the duct tape on his mouth. As Louis grips the jagged knife firmly, he tries to say something on top of his own scream. "I'm sorry, buddy," I think is what he says.

Slayer points the barrel at Louis's left temple. Without hesitation, Louis reaches to his right with his left hand, strokes the blade down against the base of Robert's penis, and slices.

Roberto's scream is incredibly painful. The duct tape can't hold his jaw shut. For about five seconds, no blood rises from the wound. Then, it starts squirting everywhere, spraying in every direction. A stream of blood runs down Robert's thighs. The lesion sprays everything from ceiling to floor. Blood streams off the couch and puddles onto the floor.

Louis holds the severed, dripping dick that drips blood from both sides, and cries, "Are you happy now, fucker!"

During all of the commotion, Yeval does his usual clapping and bouncing while cracking up.

Slayer is laughing with Yeval.

"That was good, wasn't it Yeval?" laughs out Slayer.

"Yes," Yeval says. "Now make him eat it."

Slayer stops laughing. He thinks for a minute and then turns to Louis and says, "Eat it."

"No, not that one," says Yeval. "The other one. Make him eat his own penis."

"Yes, perfect," Slayer says. "Feed it to him."

Slayer still points the gun at Louis.

Louis tears the tape off of Roberto. Roberto's face is white and his eyes are closed. Louis tries to slip the penis in Roberto's mouth, but when Louis opens Roberto's jaw, it just hangs open.

"He won't eat it," Louis says.

Louis chokes on his vomit and coughs it out all over Roberto's lap.

Slayer fires the gun between Roberto's eyes.

Roberto's forehead caves in, and blood drips from his nose, now swollen. Roberto's eyes open slightly and then close. He's died.

"You eat it," Slayer demands of Louis.

Louis closes his eyes, takes a deep breath, and bites into the head of the penis. He bites about half way through it before he starts moaning in frustration.

"It's too rough."

"Make him cook it," Yeval says.

"No," Slayer says to Yeval. "I should get going. The police are probably on their way."

Slayer snatches the knife from Louis, who doesn't put up a struggle. Slayer stabs his finger into the wound where Roberto's penis used to be, and wets his finger with an artery still dripping blood. He writes on the coffee table in front of us, "SLAYER".

Slayer throws the knife and gun into his bag and heads for the fire escape. As he exits, he turns around and addresses Morgan and Louis, both of whom are in extreme shock, and says, "Make sure to thank Randy. He's the reason I didn't kill you two."

Slayer looks into my eyes, and I glare back at him. What did he mean by that? Why did he leave three out of four of us alive? Does he want something? He smiles at me and winks.

"I'll see you again, Randy," he says and disappears into the night.

CHAPTER 26

# Morgan

The police arrive at my apartment twenty minutes after Slayer departed. Ambulances block the street as the three of us survivors are rushed to the hospital. I am checked by doctors, physically and psychologically. "How did you feel when you saw Roberto being penectomized?" or "Did you think you were going to die?" It didn't really help that much. After the doctors had examined me, the police had questions of their own.

Lime and Curtis arrived at the hospital a couple hours after us. By that time, I was eating some soup and being cross-examined by four men who said they were with the police.

"Don't answer anymore questions, Randy," Curtis says, entering the room with Lime.

"We'll take it from here, gentlemen," says Lime.

Without argument, the officers leave.

I give Curtis and Lime the full run through of what happened. Lime is too wrapped up in the whole penectomy thing that he doesn't even absorb the most important fact of all...Yeval and Slayer were communicating with each other.

"Slayer sees Yeval too," I say to Lime.

"Randy, Yeval is just in your mind," says Curtis. "Now enough with the small talk. What was he wearing?"

"All black. His face painted white."

"And?"

"And I couldn't make out who he was."

Curtis sighs. It makes me feel pathetic.

"What! It was hard to make out any characteristics when his face is covered in paint. I could tell by the structure he must have been Caucasian, and older. That's about it."

"That's all you can help us out with, Randy?" Lime says. I sense any unfriendliness from Lime for the first time. "He was standing right next to you."

133

"Well, I'm sorry I couldn't help more, Marlon, but I was in a fucked up situation," I say. He is shaking his head as I say this.

Lime sighs. "I understand," he says, though I know he doesn't mean it.

"I don't know," I say. "Do you understand? Do you know what it's like to have your teeth knocked out by some gangsters, or watch a serial killer make someone else eat a severed penis? I don't think you do understand."

"Tell me about..." Lime begins.

"No, I am done answering questions for today," I yell. "I know what you want to know and I've given you my best."

The lights are dimmed, and the faint glow shines off of Lime's face as he looks at me in frustration. I see this look too often. Now that another person I care about has given me this look, I feel like I'll always be a disappointment.

"Just leave." I wave them off.

"I'm not here as just a detective, I'm here as a friend." Lime reassures.

"I don't want to talk to you and I'm not your friend."

Lime looks down at the floor, then looks up at Curtis. "Fine," he says to me without eye contact. "Come on," he tells Curtis.

An hour later I am wandering up and down the third floor looking for Morgan. I find her laying in a hospital bed, talking with the same police officers who were questioning me (but they're nicer to her).

I eavesdrop for a few minutes until I hear Caroline's voice from across the hall. I run over and hug her tight. I figured that at a time like this, I'd be happiest to see her, the most important person in my life. But I'm not. I'm actually more concerned with Morgan.

"My God, baby, are you okay?" she asks me. I smile at her revealing my missing front tooth and she doesn't ask anymore questions.

The police leave Morgan's room and head down the hall to, I'm assuming, Louis's room.

"I love you..." I begin to tell Caroline.

"I love you too," she interrupts.

"...But you'll have to excuse me for a few minutes," and I walk into Morgan's room, not realizing how much of an ungrateful prick I am being to Caroline. But I have an excuse, I'm crazy and in shock.

I enter Morgan's room and close the door behind me. She's by herself watching *Jeopardy!* even though she doesn't know any of the answers/questions.

She looks over and sees me. I can't describe the look on her face, but it's obvious she wasn't expecting to see me.

"Hello Morgan," I say smugly, as I make my way to the window. "How are we feeling? Peachy, I hope."

"I'll never get over this," she says. "You have no idea."

"Oh, I think I do," I respond. Without giving her a chance to respond, I continue, "Maybe your precious eyes wouldn't have had to witness such an event if you didn't break into my apartment in the first place."

She swallows (no pun intended).

"Yes, that's right Morgan," I continue. "The Seattle Slayer went to my apartment to save me. What were you, Roberto, and Louis going to do to me? Huh?"

The cunt doesn't answer.

"I see. Well, am I to tell the police when they question me that I was in the middle of being robbed when the Seattle Slayer entered?"

She still doesn't answer.

"I won't tell them, if you tell me what the fuck you were doing in my apartment."

I feel powerful.

"We were there to take what money you have left stashed," she says.

"Don't lie to me, bitch," I say heartlessly. "You know damn well I don't have money."

"No, it's the truth Randy," she says, shaking her head stupidly. "I hear you talking about pearls and rubies in your sleep all the time."

I look out the window at all the cars sitting in traffic, just waiting. How much of our lives do we waste just waiting? How much are we polluting our planet while we wait in traffic? Does anybody care? No. Would anybody care if I died? No. I should just jump out the window right now.

I bang my hand on the glass loudly, startling Morgan.

I scream, "Goddamnit, Morgan. All of this because of something you heard while I was sleeping! Pearls? Rubies? That's it? You take two dangerous men, men that cut off my toe no less, break into my home and assault me, assuming you might get some jewelry."

Again, she doesn't respond.

"You're a whore. This is all because of you."

I walk back to the door, then stop myself as I turn the knob.

"Humans waste so much time in life," I say, staring at the door. "Arguing. Driving. *Relationships.* I wasted two years of my life with you. I took care of you. I loved you. What did I get in return, Morgan? Nothing."

I turn around to look at her. There are tears in her eyes, but they are not for me.

"I don't ever want to see you again. Don't stop by the house. Don't call. Don't email. You are dead to me."

Though what I'm saying is true and it satisfies my rage toward the bitch, I do still love her for some retarded reason. I did want to take care of her. I did try and change her for the better. But it didn't work. She's worse than before. Unremorseful. I am just another dildo to Morgan. She is just something else I failed at.

"When I get the money, I'll mail you a $500 check to your grandmother's house. That will replace whatever you stole from her credit card, as well as helping you get on your feet. I don't actually expect you to use it to pay your grandmother back, so, hopefully you will spend it wisely."

I realize that I am being no better than Morgan is. Because she has hurt me, I am trying hurting her back. But that's not how I want her to remember me.

I put my anger aside.

"Goodbye, my Morgan. I will miss you. There was a time when I did love you. But you broke my heart.

"I wish you the best. Goodbye," and with that, I look at her beautiful face one last time, wishing that beauty wasn't just on the outside, open the door and exit.

I never see or hear from Morgan or Louis again. I heard Morgan works as a waitress near Alki and is in drug-rehab. Good for her. Samuel, an old buddy and ex-customer of mine, says he saw her at her grandmother's house when he went to deliver a package for the neighbors. He said she looks good as always, but less hootchie. I don't know whether that's hot or not. Whatever.

Louis, I heard, committed suicide three months later by piercing both of his forearms with a knife. His home-dawgs found him in bed, though I heard he lost a lot of his homies after word got out what Slayer made him do to Roberto. I guess he lost his dominance by choosing his own life over his homie's. But about a month after I heard Louis died, I saw a most-wanted sign for a guy who looked like him. It was a surveillance-photograph of him (or a man looking like him) robbing a bank. I tried to look up his death in old newspapers while I was at the library and asked a couple of his old time gangsters what became of him. Nothing was official, as most of the people had their own story of when they last saw Louis. Him being alive or dead shouldn't matter to me, since he attempted to kill me more than once. I don't know why I care what came of him. He'll be dead one day if he's not now. Even if he is alive, he knows better than to ever fuck with me.

This is the end of my relationship with two people who played major parts in my life during my later twenties. But this isn't the end of my story.

Like Lime said, life just keeps going…

CHAPTER 27

# Interview

"The intersection of Aurora and 130<sup>th</sup> Street will be closed until the seventh. Police and construction will be rebuilding the overpass that collapsed, leaving nobody injured. Back to you, Matt," reports some blonde bimbo on the evening news.

"Thank you, Janis. Now we take you to Eva Thomson with our top story. An interview with Randy Mulray, a survivor of the Seattle Slayer. Eva..." says Matt, some douche-bag in has late forties attempting to look like a twenty-something. He has dark brunette hair, though I wouldn't be surprised to find out that only half of it is real.

I sit in a blue chair facing Eva Thomson, some black hardbody news anchor for KATO 12, one of our local news station. I am their top story and they want to know *all* about my attack. We are in a secluded room that has just three chairs and some lights. There are about eight of us.

The blue chair I am sitting in was at my request. The original chair was red, but I wouldn't sit in it because it reminded me too much of the Dark Room. I got my way by saying, "It reminds me too much of a bad place I was in. I'm already reliving something bad that's happened to me, please don't make me relive something else." I was probably more of a bitch about it, because I did refuse to do the interview unless they got me a different colored chair. One of the nice people on set offered a cozy-looking white chair, but the fat balled gaffer exclaimed, "But it won't look good in the picture." This whole interview is more trouble than it's worth, but Caroline and Ryan, who are watching me at the back of the room, are excited for me.

"Thank you, Matt," says Eva.

Here we go.

"I am sitting here live with Randy Mulray, a twenty-nine year old Seattle resident."

I look at the monitor a couple feet behind Eva's head and can see myself on it. I'm on television. Cool.

"Only three days ago, Randy and his friends were attacked and assaulted by the notorious Seattle Slayer."

Eva looks at me.

"Randy, thank you for joining us tonight."

"You're welcome," I say, toneless.

"Randy, tell us about what you experienced on Tuesday evening?"

"Well, long story short, I was being robbed by three acquaintances of mine, when the Seattle Slayer appeared out of nowhere. He then tied the three intruders at gunpoint, and made one of the guys mutilate the other guy."

I can see the gap from my missing tooth as I glance back and forth at the monitor. I'm getting it fixed next week. However, it doesn't look too bad. I wonder if it's unattractive. I should ask Caroline.

"You were being robbed?"

"Yes."

Eva can sense that I don't have any more to say about that, so she moves on. "How are you coping with what has happened to you."

"Well, I'm just thankful I guess."

"Thankful," she says. "In what way?"

"I'm thankful that I'm alive, I'm thankful that I didn't get my dick chopped off…"

"Randy," she interrupts quickly. "You can't say that on the air."

"My apologies. I'm thankful my penis didn't get chopped off…"

"Whoa, Randy," she says. "We're live."

"So? It's what happened."

"But there are certain things you're not allowed to say," she conveys.

"So you're censoring something that really happened," I ask. "That's not news."

"We're not *censoring*, but there are certain details the public doesn't need to know."

"How do you presume? If you don't deliver news for what it actually is, then it's not the news. It's fucking reality T.V."

Someone yells cut.

"I'm not listening to this," Eva says. "Back to you, Matt."

"No, wait a minute, I have a story to tell," I say.

They don't listen. I see that monitor behind Eva goes back to Matt.

"Bullshit!" I scream.

Eva looks at me as if I'm nothing but trashed, as if this anger has come from nowhere, and tears the microphone off her dress.

People are talking in the room.

"You will listen to my story," I yell at Eva as she is getting up.

The whole room freezes and shuts the fuck up.

"You fucking reporters do nothing but glamorize violence," I say. "It's nothing but fucking murder this, and rape that. You report that there is an armed and dangerous man one night, but don't even fucking bother to update us the next night. You fucking people have warped our society into being scared of everyone. And now, when something to really worry about is out there, you soften the truth. You make it entertainment. Who's Slayer going to kill next!? Who's the man they know as Slayer!? It's bullshit. You guys are giving him what he wants. You guys are presenting him as a villain, rather than a menace. He is dangerous, and will not stop until he is dead."

Eva, sitting back down now, remains silent.

Seconds go by until someone finally responds to me...

"Asshole!"

"Hey," says Eva. "He's right."

"This isn't 'Man bites dog', Eva," I tell her. "When you're doing a story on the Seattle Slayer, it's 'Dog *neuters* man'."

Caroline, Ryan, and I walk out in the hallway. My father sits out there waiting for us.

"That was a very nice interview, Randy," says my father sarcastically.

"It was cool," Ryan says. "I liked it when you were mad. You were right, Randy."

Caroline been able to take that grin off her face.

"Too bad no one will listen," I say.

"I understand where you're coming from," says Eva, entering the hallway. "What you said was bright. Why don't you write down what you experienced and your opinion of the entire case, and get it to me. Maybe I can help your voice get heard."

"I'm not in it for the money," I say proudly.

"Randy," Eva says to me. "Turning something negative into a positive isn't selfish. It's just making the best of a bad situation. It's life." She then walks off.

I never realized, but it is true. I try to contradict that logic the entire car ride home, but I can't. Maybe I should take advantage of the bad things in life. Perhaps take advantage of knowing this killer so well that I can expose him, which will increase the chances of him being stopped. The police may not understand me, but maybe the public will.

I call Eva, who gave me her card, when I get home. I apologize to her, and she tells me that I didn't need to. I also agree to write down everything I think is important about my experience. She agrees to have lunch with me next week after I get my tooth fixed.

As I sit and write on my computer, my phone beeps. It tells me that I have a voice-message. I go to the menu and remember that my ringer was on silent for the interview.

The voice message was sent less than two minutes ago. It's from Detective Lime.

"Randy, it's Marlon. Listen, I decided to look into a storage garage I found under George Curtis's name. I can't say much else, but I need you here as soon as possible. The address is 30630 47th Street North, Yourself Storage, storage room 7E. Call me as soon as you get this."

As I am about to call, I hear the triangle. Yeval appears behind me. The Pearl floats only a few inches from where I sit.

"You can either help Lime or save a victim" Yeval says. "You can't do both. Which do you choose?"

I know I have to move quickly, so I go with my first instinct. I grab onto the Pearl and enter the Dark Room.

The screen is dark, all except for a little crack of light. As my eyes adjust, I see that the blackness is actually boxes, and the crack of light is what Slayer can see in between the boxes.

My eyes adjust even better and I can make out that there is a figure moving around. It's a person. Slayer is hiding from a person. Slayer looks down at his hand, gripping the same knife that Louis used on Roberto.

Suddenly, someone switches the lights on and Slayer is startled. He looks around, and I see that he's hiding behind boxes piled in a storage unit. He peeks though the boxes again.

I see who Slayer is hiding from.

He's hiding from Detective Lime.

## CHAPTER 28

# Lime

"Where is it?" I scream at Yeval.

"You'll never find it," he says.

I crawl along the floor, searching thoroughly for the ruby.

"Freeze!" I hear Lime yell. "Turn around and put your hands up." Lime has him!

I stop and watch the screen.

Slayer doesn't listen. He just stares at Lime.

"Put the knife down, turn around, and put your hands on you head," Lime screams again.

"I like you, Lime," says Slayer. "But it's either me or you."

Lime's face gives a confused look. Slayer suddenly steps forward and chucks the knife. It turns two times, and pierces Lime in the right peck before he gets a chance to move.

Slayer walks up and pulls the knife. A thick stream of blood drips from the wound. Slayer checks Lime's pockets for other weapons. He then rushes to the storage door and closes it.

"You're a coward," Lime says, still strong. "You have to cover your face."

"Who am I, Lime?" Slayer says. Lime doesn't answer. "Come on, the papers made fun of Randy for not being able to identify me. Is the paint really that misleading?"

"Yes, it is," says Lime. "He was right, George. The paint is misleading."

Blood slips through Lime's hand, which hold his wound.

"You're nothing but a coward," he says, gasping.

Slayer digs in a box and takes out an old mirror. He looks at himself in it and smiles. "Of course the paint is misleading," he says. "Why else would I wear it? To look like a clown?"

Slayer takes some paper towels from a box and a water bottle from another.

"I enjoy hiding out in here while I think of my family," says Slayer. "That's why I have all these utilities, along with the evidence you were looking for."

Slayer pops the cap off of the bottle and pours the water onto his head. He wipes his drenched face off with several paper towels. The screen goes black as he daps his eyes. When he removes the towels, Lime's head is shaking.

"Why, George?" asks Lime.

Slayer looks at himself in the mirror. There is still paint on his face, but you can tell who he is. Just as I thought all along.

"You'll find evidence here," says Slayer. "But nothing incriminating. That's all someplace else. You're not sitting on a gold mine, Marlon, though I do have to give you props for tracking me down. Why on earth did you think to test my fingerprints?"

The Seattle Slayer is obviously Detective George Curtis, and I feel a sudden frustration because nobody believed me.

"George, I know that not all the prints match," Lime says. "You're not alone. We know that. Okay? Now, tell us who did it and they'll spare you the death penalty."

"No, no, no," says Curtis. "I'm not going to get caught."

"Yes, you will," Lime says confidently. "This is *your* parking garage. Plus, Randy is on his way. He'll help me foil your plan and bring you in. Just tell us who your partner is."

"Randy? Crazy Randy?" says Curtis. "Tell me, Marlon, if Randy is on his way, then why is he on the floor of the Dark Room looking for the ruby?" Curtis looks in the mirror and smiles. He's smiling at me. He was smiling at me all along.

"Yeval, where's the fucking ruby?" I cry, begging for his help. I moan and cry as I crawl along the dark floor.

I look over at Yeval and notice that he's gone. I look up at the screen and see Curtis tying Lime to a fold out chair, while Yeval watches and laughs in the corner.

"You little bastard," I yell at the screen.

"I'm going to have fun with you," Curtis says.

I look closely at the bump in the smooth dark floor and see the ruby lodged in the black wooded floor.

"You shoved the ruby in it, you bastard," I say to Yeval.

Yeval just laughs, "See how fast you can get here. Can you do it in time?"

It takes me three and a half minutes and four fingernails until I am able to dig the ruby out. I look up at the screen before grabbing the ruby and see that Curtis is punching Lime in the face.

There is still time.

"Now cut him in the…" I hear Yeval start to say as I grab on to the ruby.

I am returned to my room. I slip on a pair of shoes and grab a kitchen knife, then run down to the garage. Opening my car door I see that all of the fingernails on my right hand, except the pinky, have been scratched to nothing. Blood seeps and burns, but I am still able to grab the knife firmly as I haul ass to Yourself Storage Unit.

I drive my car right up to the entrance of Yourself Storage, throwing it in park and then turning it off. After releasing the keys from the ignition, the inside alarm beeps when I open the door because I haven't turned the headlights off; but I am in no position to be concerned with that. I ignore the alert and run out of my car to the entrance, which is an electric sliding door that is open to customers twenty four hours a day.

There is an elevator right next to the entrance. I press the button for the seventh floor. The elevator door opens and I run for unit 7E. I stand there and stare at the closed entrance. I put my right ear against the vertical aluminum door and listen carefully. There is no sound. I look down, seeing a lock and a handle on the middle of it.

I take the knife I brought with my left hand because it isn't sore like my right hand is. As I grab the door handle with the right hand, I begin to have split feelings about this situation. One side of me hopes the door is unlocked, so I can catch Curtis and save Lime. Another part of me wants it to be locked so I can guard the outside while I call the police. This thought reminds me that I forgot to take my cell phone when I left, being in the hurry that I was. Goddmanit.

I take a deep breath, and then I pull the handle. The door is unlocked. I slide the door open and blindly thrust the knife under the door just in case Curtis is standing near by on the other side.

The door is open, and I see no trace of Curtis or Yeval. I am too late. Lime sits in the fold out chair, dead and naked.

I walk in and take a closer look.

Lime's eyes have been gouged out, his stomach cut open with intestines hanging out, and his genitals have been cut off and shoved in his mouth. When I see his liver on the floor I can't look any longer.

I run out of Yourself, across the street to a grocery store where I mumble at a cashier that I have obviously made nervous.

After she deciphers my thick stuttering, "Cccalll the pppppppppooooo-lice," the police arrive to the grocery store, where I am able to tell them what I have discovered in the storage unit across the street.

Shortly later, detectives come to question me. I sit in the employee room at the grocery store and tell them that I won't speak to anyone except Chief Harold Milton.

"Do you want a lawyer?" one of the detectives asks me. He has a mustache and is a little overweight. He has a wedding ring on, but he looks like a pervert, so I assume he looks at a lot of pornography.

"No, ugly," I say, very angry. "Get Chief Milton over here now, or you're going to have trouble."

They contemplate whether or not to take me in. However, Chief Milton happens to be looking for me, so they decide to give me my way.

I am taken back to the police station where I agree only to talk with Milton in his office.

"It was George?" responds Chief after I tell him. "Yeah, right. You are crazy."

"You have to trust me," I say gently, hoping that Chief Milton will believe me.

"I think you're crazy and I don't care what you say," he says.

I can't think of anything else to say.

"But," he continues, "I am going to question Curtis and have him fingerprinted anyway."

What I assume is going on is that either Milton doesn't want to admit that I'm right, or he's going to sabotage evidence to make it look like Curtis isn't partners with him. It makes so much sense.

"Well, I think the truth will come out when the results get back," I say, standing, and heading for the door.

"I hope your wrong," Chief says. "I have known that man for thirty years. He lost his family in a fire. Two children and a wife. He's been through a lot, but still, I can't imagine him doing such terrible things."

"I know I'm right, Chief. It doesn't surprise me that his family is dead, either. In fact, it sounds awfully convenient."

As Chief's eyes widen. I immediately exit, avoiding anymore trouble.

I am dropped back to my car by one of the deputies. I cry on the way home and it makes the deputy very uneasy. I feel horrible because Detective Lime was the only one who believed me. He was the only one who trusted me. The only one who understood me. And now he's gone. I am all alone.

I put the keys in the lock of my apartment and remember that I left it unlocked again. I search every corner of the house with another kitchen knife, because the police took mine. I don't find anyone though.

I go to the kitchen and pour myself a drink, well actually, just some straight vodka. When I take a seat on the stool at my kitchen counter I see an envelope. There is red smear on the closing of it and contains something in it. I rip the envelope open and out falls a severed tongue.

I jump out of the stool in shock and I start gagging. After a couple of minutes when I finally get my senses together, I notice that the envelope contained something else too…a Polaroid. I pull the picture out, which is also covered in blood, and look at it.

This whole situation has just gotten worse. The picture is of a woman tied up, crying, and covered in blood. When I look closely, there is no doubt in my mind who it is. Caroline.

CHAPTER 29

# Curtis

I was able to find Curtis's home address through the help of the internet. I drove to his home strapped with two handguns, a grenade I bought from a guy named Leroy and a digital camera I got from Ryan last Christmas.

While driving to Curtis's residence, I cut all stops signs, ran several red lights, and dented the shit out of my car.

Upon my arrival, I break a window and crawl through to get inside the house. I try and try to kick the door down, but it won't budge. When I finally break in, I discover that it had been bolted shut from the inside. Why? Because Curtis knows that *I* gathered the evidence to link him to the crime.

Where is he now? Gone for good? Lime's body was found in his storage space, so it's a no-brainer he's a killer.

"You'll find nothing in there," says Yeval, sitting in a chair at the dining room table. "He wouldn't leave anything behind."

I don't bother acknowledging Yeval. I am too distracted and too worried about Caroline to give a shit about what Yeval thinks.

"You can see inside his head, so he can see inside of yours," Yeval reminds me.

As I open the oak hut that has wine glasses, crystals, and china made God knows when, Yeval yells at me not to destroy anything. Apparently, it was Curtis's wife's dining collection.

"Fuck you," I say to Yeval, and then start throwing the glasses and dishes everywhere.

"George is going to be angry," says Yeval.

I look over at Yeval who is shaking his head at me while I continue breaking shit. Not paying attention, I cut the entire pinky side of my right hand on the edge of a plate I broke against the cupboard. It's the fifth time this year something has happened to my right hand.

I continue annihilating Curtis's cozy home, which has obviously been cleaned to hide something. I destroy the garage, the kitchen, the study, the living room, the bathroom, and finally the two bedrooms and I don't find shit. I even go through the trash, the yard waste, even the glass (where I cut my hand again).

I calm myself, go back inside, wrap my hand up, and splash cool water on my face to get my senses back.

Preparing to leave, I take one last look around the house, making sure I destroyed everything. I literally destroyed everything. So I leave.

As I exit the house and walk toward my car, I see a recycle bin with Curtis's address on it, sitting out on the side walk. I knock it over for fun, and a bunch of papers fall out. Lucky for me, it's not a windy day or else what I found in the recycle what have instantly been blown away.

I find a piece of paper with the address: "1971 Clifton Road SW". So, I drive there.

Hauling ass down the interstate I dial 0 on my cell phone.

"Operator," says the high pitch male voice.

"Yes, I need to be connected to the Seattle Police Department immediately. It's an emergency."

As I am being connected, I drive past the mall and remember that I still don't have Sublime's *40 Ounces to Freedom* in my album collection. I should probably also pick up a Gordon Lightfoot album too; a greatest hits compilation would probably be satisfactory. Come to think of it, I need an obscure rap CD in my collection. Brotha Lynch Hung's *EBK4*, Mac 10's self-titled debut, Eminem's *Infinite*, or Immortal Technique's *Revolutionary Volume 2* should be in order.

"Seattle Police Department," says a po-po over the phone.

"Get me Chief Milton," I say professionally, yet demanding.

They transfer me to his office where his phone rings six times. On the seventh ring the answering machine picks up: "You have reached the voice mailbox of Police Chief Harold Milton. Please leave a message and I will return your call at my earliest convenience. If this is an emergency, hang up now and dial 911. To schedule an appointment, dial 1 to be transferred to my secretary. Otherwise, stay on the line. Thank you." Beep.

"Chief Milton, it's Randy Mulray. Listen, uh," I realize I don't know what to say. "I need your help. I know you think I'm crazy. But, I also know that you think I'm right. You haven't been able to contradict a single thing

I have said, so…listen the fuck up. I got a new lead, and you're my only hope. Please be there for me. Get to 1971 Clifton Road SW as fast as you can. Drop your shit because this is critical. 1971 Clifton Road SW."

Clifton Road is a place I am familiar with because it overlooks Alki Beach. Many places in the area do, but Clifton Road is a rundown area. I got my meth in the area all the time about eight years ago. I'd go to the clinic down the street from Sam and take condoms. I'd shoot myself up, and then pass out on the park bench that overlooked the beach. The view would remind me of when my mother used to take me to Alki. But sometimes it would remind me of the accident, and if I was high I would try to stumble back to Sam's and buy some more smack so I could overdose and die.

I freewheel my ride, dented though still pimped, past 1971 Clifton Road to see what it is like. It is a warehouse or a factory. There is a Jeep Cherokee parked outside of it. I park my car down the block from the warehouse. I check my pockets to make sure I have my guns, my grenade, my keys, and my cell phone. I naturally lock my car with a remote on my key-chain, which makes an obnoxious beeping noise that can be heard for miles. I figure that I should've manually locked the car, for fear that I might have drawn attention to myself. I usually never lock my door, but I did now because the last thing I want is someone breaking into my car. No, actually the last thing I want is for Caroline to be suffering. Come to think of it, my car is just a possession, and it shouldn't mean shit to me at all.

Conveniently, the warehouse's front door is unlocked. I enter, scanning every corner of the warehouse before I shut the door. The warehouse is large, empty, and has four doors including the entrance. One door leads to an office with a window on the second floor. I know this because I can see through the window from the bottom floor.

I walk up the stairs, which are about to collapse, and look into the office. It is empty. As I carefully walk down the stairway, I overlook the warehouse. It looks so lonely and forgotten—brought into the world with a purpose to do something, but failed. Like me. Why was this large place built? My mind is distracted by the depressing setting of the cold empty warehouse.

Under the stairway, where the two doors are, Curtis walks out.

"Hey, motherfucker," I yell at him as I jump off the wobbling stairway. Curtis looks up at me and runs into the next room as I jump.

Instead of chasing after him, I open the door of the room he just came out of. Inside is a bunch of tools. I am tempted to use my grenade to blow it all up, but out of fear that the grenade might take this whole warehouse down and kill us all, I refrain from using it.

Both my guns are cocked and loaded. I stick one of them in my jeans. I open the door, pull out the pistol held in my waist, and point both guns in front of me. Entering the room, I see a light.

This particular room reminds me of the Dark Room. But it's not. It's much different. Nothing about it is the same, actually. It just reminds me of the Dark Room because I have the same nervous feeling I do when in the Dark Room.

The room is big, maybe a hundred by a hundred feet. Caroline sits in a chair, bloodied, battered, and tied up. It doesn't look like she's been touched though since that photograph was taken. There is an empty chair to the right of her, and to the left stands Curtis, pointing a gun at me. Yeval stands next to Curtis. Caroline's mouth is taped shut and her eyes and nose are drenched with tears and mucus.

"Hello, Randy," says Yeval.

"Hello, Randy," says Curtis.

"Hello, Randy," says a familiar voice from behind me. I turn to see who it is. I see a club come at me and I am knocked out cold.

I awake minutes later to find myself tied up next to Caroline.

CHAPTER 30

# Showdown

"Wake up," The figure in front of me says, as his hand flies across my face, smacking me.

To the left, I hear Caroline sobbing. My sweetheart must be so scared right now.

I focus and find myself in the same room as I last remember, tied to a chair next to Caroline's. My hands and feet are tied with the same cable ties that Curtis tied Tracey to the bed with. Caroline and I are tied together by rope wrapped around our arms. My mouth isn't duct-taped shut like Caroline's is. They want me to talk.

Yeval sits on a wooden tool bench tapping his long fingernails on the surface. He smiles at me and says, "You're screwed."

On Yeval's workbench are my guns and grenade. This is a toolbox with either tools or torture devices (or both) in it, and rubbing alcohol and gasoline both sit on the ground beneath Yeval's feet. I look around the room and notice that there is a bathtub in the corner.

"He's awake!" yells Yeval.

"You're a cocksucker," I say to Yeval.

"Don't hate me, I'm just a figment of your imagination, right?" he says. I hear someone walking closer and closer. "Here they come."

*They?*

The door opens and Curtis walks in.

"Where's you know who?" Yeval asks Curtis.

"He's coming," says Curtis. "Randy, sorry my accomplice had to hit you over the head. But if you were to shoot me, that'd ruin everything."

"Why didn't you guys just kill me?" I ask. "You want to torture me more, you cocksuckers? Well, here I am."

I don't know why I am encouraging these assholes to fuck me up even more. I think it's because I hope to look tough in front of Caroline.

"Because that would ruin everything too, Randy," Curtis says.

"I hope that you have the longest, most agonizing death anybody has ever endured," I say.

"You see," says Curtis. "Even people who don't kill, like you, still wish to see others die. Isn't that a bit hypocritical?"

"You kill the innocent," I say.

"Oh, everybody is guilty of something or another, Randy. Look at you. You're a no good drug dealer who can't possibly appreciate anything about life because you're caught up in the past. What good is being alive if you can't appreciate it? I might as well do you the favor and kill you. Or maybe I should teach you a *real* lesson and kill something you really do appreciate." He looks over at Caroline.

"I called the police, they're on their way," I say, trying to turn Curtis's attention away from Caroline.

"No you didn't," Yeval says.

"Are you sure?" I ask Yeval.

"Please Randy," Curtis says. "Wouldn't the police be here by now if you really called them?"

Yes. Perhaps I should've called the police instead of just calling Chief. Yet, another stupid thing I've done.

"Yes," Yeval answers for me.

"And wouldn't they question your phone call?" says Curtis.

"Yes," Yeval says.

"I mean, after all, how many times have you reported you saw the actual Seattle Slayer?" Curtis says, approaching me. He leans down so he's eye to eye with me. "You didn't call the police. I know it."

"You're screwed, Randy," Yeval says. "Join us or you and Caroline die."

"Fuck you," I say.

"Don't you understand, Randy," Curtis says, running his finger softly down the blade. "You're one of us. Yeval is a gift. Yeval is your friend. And your life will be much better if you listen to him."

"My life would be much better if I'm a killer?" I say sarcastically. "You know they're after you, Curtis."

"Yes. And the world will remember me," he says.

"Yeah, as a fucking psycho," I reply quickly.

"It just goes to show that hatred is more effective than praise. That's what I want. I want to be remembered as something. Anybody can be a hero. And what happens to heroes, Randy? They get forgotten in a day. While monsters, they're remembered forever. Dahmer, Bundy, Manson, Gacy, *Jack the Ripper*—they'll be remembered and studied for years and years. I will be a legend," he says.

"That's it?" I ask condescendingly, though I can only imagine how pathetic I look talking shit while I'm tied to a chair. "That's your motive?" I'm disappointed. I thought Slayer was deeper than that.

"No, my friend, that is not what we stand for," says a voice I recognize.

In walks Dr. Jenkins.

"Hello Randy," Jenkins says walking into the room with a teapot and a funnel. "Let me ask you this, Randy," he says as he walks toward the work bench. "I spent my whole youth studying to become a therapist. I spent years, into my thirties counseling those who needed my help. I was a good therapist, wasn't I?"

"You were okay, I guess."

"You see. 'Okay.' I was very good," he says. "And I helped many people. But I never got recognition for any of it. So, one day, I took my anger out on a hooker I picked up on Main Street. That's when I noticed that murder would get me recognition."

Caroline budges aggressively for a second, then sits still again.

"I was amazed at how big of a deal the police made after the discovery of *just* a dead hooker," Jenkins continues. "I was also amazed at how good it felt killing another human being. Why not do something you enjoy and get recognition for it?"

"It is such a great feeling, Randy," says Curtis. "To have such control over something so delicate. To destroy something so precious."

"George came to me," Jenkins says, "Oh, gosh, mid-sixties?" he asks Curtis.

"Sounds about right."

"Curtis was a patient of mine," Jenkins tells me. "He came to me after his family was killed in a fire. He said he felt it was all his fault because he left the oven on and was the only one to survive. Well, sure enough a demon named Yeval told him that he killed his family on purpose. He wasn't sure how to feel about the situation, so after months and months of me counseling Curtis and getting into his head, I finally convinced him to kill someone and see how he liked it. Sure enough, George and I picked up a hooker together, took her to a motel, and just fucking tore her apart, limb by limb."

"They never found that one. Shit, I can't even remember what we did with the body," says Curtis, laughing.

"I think we cooked the flesh off on my stove, and then threw away the bones," he says. "The police were looking for that particular prostitute because she had been a missing person since the day after we murdered her."

During Jenkins babbling, I notice that Caroline's deep gasping has stopped. I turn to look to see if she is okay and I notice she is as still as a statue.

"Caroline," I say softly over Jenkins's talking. She doesn't respond. Because of the graphic details Jenkins and Curtis are providing, she must assume they're going to do the same to her.

"Why are you telling me this?" I shout. "I don't care. I don't care for your explanation. I find it cowardly. So why are you telling me this?"

Jenkins stops and stares at me. Curtis looks at Jenkins for direction.

"I'm telling you this because," Jenkins tells me, "the idea of you knowing all the details before you are killed fills me with pleasure. The look in the victim's eyes when they know the shallow selfish reasoning behind their death is so fulfilling. I want to see that look in your eyes, Randy."

"Explain Yeval to me," I say. "That's what I want to know. Why do Curtis and I both see Yeval, but nobody else does."

"Yeval is something you both created on your own, through the guilt that continuously haunted you day and night," he explains. "It's called telepathy. You and George communicate by mind. Though most people would imagine you two communicate personally through the act of talking to each other inside your head, you two actually communicate through the creature you built separately."

"Why can I see in his mind, but he can't see in mine," I ask. Right now my main concern should be getting brutally murdered, but I just have to know.

"Oh, I can see you too, Randy," says Curtis, his ugly old balding ass smirking so smugly at me, tied helplessly to a chair. "I've been inside the Dark Room many times."

"What did you see?" I ask.

"Every time Yeval was standing there taunting you, I was watching," he says to me. "Every time he'd appear to you, I'd enter the Dark Room by grabbing the Pearl. We are inside each other's minds. We are in the middle of our own heaven and hell." He comes up to me and puts the knife to my neck, saying, "The Dark Room may be a hell to you, but it is heaven to me.

"I know you well, Randy. I understand you. I know the pain you are going through. Give in to Yeval as I did and I promise you the pain will go away."

"But Yeval is still in you, he's right there," I nod my head to where Yeval sits on the workbench. For the first time he is as quiet as a cat.

"You will learn from Jenkins and I that Yeval is here to guide you, not to torment you," Curtis says, as he starts to untie my hands.

"George, what are you doing?" Jenkins asks.

"You were right, Dwight, I do understand why you had me keep him alive," Curtis says. "He is one of us."

"Don't untie him, George," Jenkins says.

"But..." Curtis tries to argue.

"It's not up for debate, George. Don't untie him."

"Fuck that," Curtis replies. "I'm the one who sees Yeval. Maybe I can call the shots once in a while."

"You already disobeyed me by bringing your bag of weapons to the murder scene, which destroyed our unique pattern of killing with items from the scene," Jenkins says, very upset. "You also kill your partner in a storage garage that is registered under your name."

"We should both have a say in everything," Curtis argues back.

"You're a detective. You should know that's how you leave clues behind."

"I'm so sick of your shit, Dwight," Curtis shouts, in a rage. "All I ever do is report to you what Yeval says to me. It's a Goddamn pain in the ass. You're a pain in the ass."

"I'm sorry George, but there has been a change in events," Jenkins replies, piercing Curtis in the back numerous times until he is on the ground, still.

I make an attempt to snatch the blade that Curtis still holds in his dead hand, but as I go to reach for it, Jenkins snaps handcuffs on to my reaching hand and attaches them to a pipe running through the concrete floor and the ceiling.

There is no escape for me. The only thing I am grateful for is to be in touching distance of my sweet Caroline. I grab on to the leg of the chair she's sitting on and pull her closer to me. It takes all the strength my arm (which I've been working out a lot lately) can give. I succeed in pulling her about twenty inches closer to me. I rest my head in her lap and stroke her petite arms as she cries in fear. I feel my touch give warmth and hope to Caroline, who will never again be the same if she escapes.

"I am so sorry, George," Jenkins says, appearing to be genuinely upset about what he did to his 'friend'. "We've succeeded in making our mark for decades, but now it's time for us to go...go out on top. This never would have happened if I didn't give you permission to kill on your own. I thought Yeval was enough guide, but I was wrong."

Yeval hisses, though Jenkins can't here.

Jenkins approaches me with the funnel and a tea pot filled with boiling hot water. "Open your mouth, Randy."

I raise my fist and warn him, "If you come any closer, you will take a punch."

He laughs at me. "Randy, it is over for me after this," Jenkins says, not backing away. "You stopped us. They know who we are, and I can't do this without George."

"Why," I ask.

"I just can't," he says. "Yeval told him to do things. Though he organized all of the murders and carried through with a few, I was the one who thought up our mark. He is not Slayer without me. I am not Slayer without him. We are both lost without each other. We were supposed to be bigger than Jack The Ripper. But you identified George. George would later identify me, and all the hard work we had built of the last thirty years would have gone to hell. It pretty much did. The only way to fix it is to go out with a bang. I have lost all but one grain of hope. I will spare your life if you help me, Randy."

"Go fuck yourself," I tell him.

"I kept you alive because I know you have a similar instinct to George's," he says. "I spared your life because of it. This is who you are. Yeval is your proof. I am on your side. Please."

"Fuck you."

"Fair enough. I can't make you kill. But one last proposition. If you don't help me, I will kill all three of us."

"If I accept?" I ask.

"I won't kill you, or your family."

"What about Caroline?" I ask eagerly.

"Oh, her," he says as if he forgot she was still here. "She's seen too much. I'm sorry, Randy, but I'm going to kill her no matter what."

Rage flows through my head, and Jenkins can tell.

"The best partnerships start and last with honesty. I'm just being honest, Randy. I'm going to kill her no matter what. If I were to lie, you wouldn't help me. You see," he points down at Curtis, "this is where lies get you."

I rest on a gentle reply, "I shall die with her."

"That's okay," Jenkins says. "I will be my final victim. I will burn myself alive in that bathtub after I slice wounds into my skin and bathe in rubbing alcohol. Then I will ignite myself and this whole warehouse. But first, I must force you and your pretty little girlfriend to endure the worst pain imaginable. I will pour this boiling hot water down your throat causing burns that will blister your esophagus and stomach to swell to the point where you are unable to swallow, and you will slowly die from lack of air.

"While you are suffocating, I will beat your pretty little girlfriend's face in with my bare hands. Right before she is about to die from, I will insert my penis into her bleeding toothless mouth, giving her the chance to give one last blowjob and also giving me one last chance to cum. I've done a lot of things to my victims, but I've never raped any. Rape makes a serial killer look weak. As if he doesn't have power. You see, most killers rape for power, not for pleasure. But with Caroline, I have never had such a beautiful, pure victim. I will kill her while I'm climaxing, and she will be dead once I shoot my load into her mouth. It shall be heavenly." He smiles at me.

I figure I could be strong enough to break the cuffs through the pipe. But as I pull on the pipe, hoping it will snap, I realize that there is indeed no escape for me, unless I find the key.

"Open your mouth, Randy," Jenkins tells me. "The water isn't getting any hotter."

As I begin to scream loudly, both Jenkins and I hear the squeak of the warehouse door opening. Jenkins immediately sets down the funnel and teapot, grabs the gun from the work bench, and peek out the room door. A bullet spits through the door almost hitting Jenkins, who closes it before even attempting to fire back. He digs in his pockets and locks the door from the inside.

Throwing down the gun, he dashes to the work bench and picks up the gas can. Splashing Caroline and me with gas he says bitterly, "Burning alive will be a quick death compared to what I was going to do with you. I didn't even get to share the blissful torture I had inflicted on everyone else."

Sparing some gasoline, he sprinkles a thin trail of it from us to the bathtub, sitting in the corner near the entrance to the room. Jenkins splashes the wall nearest the tub with a few strokes. He then uses the rest of the can in the bathtub which is only about three feet wide and four feet long. Though I can't see from where I sit, I imagine he could only have filled the bath with less than an inch of gasoline.

Throwing the empty gas can aside, Jenkins takes out three 10-gallon buckets, labeled "Rubbing Alcohol", from under the work bench and walks them to the bathtub where he pours them in.

"Randy, are you in there?" yells a voice that I recognize. It's Chief Milton!

"Help! Harold, I'm in here!" I cry out at the top of my lungs.

As I watch the door throb from the kick on the other side, I am startled by the five bullets Jenkins unleashes. The kicking stops. I didn't even notice Jenkins had picked up his gun again.

Everything is silent. Even Caroline's deep panting is inaudible. I only hear the sound of the air conditioning, humming softly and lowly as my girlfriend and I are being tortured to death in the hell it cools.

Jenkins walks up to me, picks up the tea pot, smiles, and says, "Can't let this go to waste, now can we." And as he says "we", he tilts the teapot he's holding in his left hand down, and water surges onto Caroline's lap and into her faded blue jeans. She squeezes her eyes shut, and sobs bravely, as hot steam, bringing sweat to Jenkins's head, rises from her lap. I begin crying helplessly, and as the teapot empties, Jenkins hammers the empty aluminum teapot into Caroline's face three or four times. The shock shows in her now soulless eyes, and he leaves her alone in agonizing silence.

As saliva drips from my lip, mucus hanging from my nose, and tears dripping off my chin, I tell my sweetheart, "You're doing very good. It's almost over. I'm so proud of you." I continue to encourage her, and as I am doing this, I prey she loses consciousness, so she doesn't have to witness the pain that Jenkins is about to put all three of us through.

I turn my attention away from Caroline after a minute or so, when I hear Jenkins moaning in a scratchy tone, "Yeah. Oh yeah. That feels good. Come on." I see him cutting himself deep all over his body. He has stripped naked and taken the scalpel to his own flesh. Cuts down his eye brows, his shoulders, chest, bicep, forearms, inner thighs, and now his toes, are all deep enough to scar. Rivulets of blood have covered him in red.

Milton begins kicking the door again. He's alive! Why'd he stop kicking? Did he get shot? Was he knocked unconscious? Did he get help?

Jenkins grabs a matchbox sitting on the workbench and walks over to the tub filled with rubbing alcohol and gasoline. He step in the bath, and screams in pain as the rubbing alcohol burns the self-inflicted cuts all over his toes. He breathes deep, fighting tears, and counts to three. On three, he lays down in the tub, and screaming, he sinks his head under the liquid. His head rises out from the alcohol and gas, and he screams loud. He tries wiping his eyes, as he can't see for shit, but it doesn't help.

Jenkins blindly grabs the matchbox sitting beside the tub. I scream, "Hurry!" as Milton continues to kick at the door. Jenkins attempts to light a match, but drops it.

The door begins to break. I yell "hurry" again, as Milton keeps kicking at the door.

Jenkins attempts to light another match, saying to me, "I'm going out on top." The match drops again.

Another kick at the door. Milton's overweight legs kick through the door. I can see him.

Jenkins grabs another match, "The world will remember me."

Chief Milton kicks again, this time the door springs opens. Right away, Milton is pointing his gun at Jenkins. I see the look of horror and disgust on Milton's face.

Trying to sound intimidating, Milton screams, "Freeze!"

Jenkins strokes the match against the matchbox, and the little match lights up.

"Shoot him," I scream at Milton.

"I am Slayer," Jenkins, says loud and proud, those his last words.

As the bullet enters his chest, the lit match drops into the tub of rubbing alcohol and gasoline. Within a half second, the bathtub and Dr. Jenkins are in flames.

Jenkins twitches violently three times while he lays in the tub of fire, cooking himself. Through the blaze, I think I can hear a faint scream.

Milton cuts Caroline loose with the scalpel covered in Jenkins's blood. Caroline stands up, using every ounce of strength against the pain in her thighs from the burns.

The room is bright with flames, and I pant aggressively as heat and toxins are sucked into my lungs.

"Fuck me, get her out," I order Chief.

"No, I will…" Caroline starts.

"Go!" I cut her off.

Tears fill Caroline's eyes as Chief pushes her out of the room with him.

"I love you," I shout loudly, my throat lumped, handcuffed to the goddamned pipe.

Jenkins has only been on fire for less than forty-five seconds. I cry, feeling sorry for myself, as I sit in a scorching hot room with two serial killers. Jenkins has been burnt alive, which is no less than what he deserves. Curtis's fat ass lays on the floor, his face down, eyes closed. If there was only some way I can get out of the back door. But I know I can't.

Through the flames burning mightily with rage, I see Yeval standing there. "You got what you want," he yells at me.

I got what I want? How is that? I'm too scared, hurt, and weak to bother shouting the question to its meaning. And as the walls Jenkins splashed with gas light up, and my eyes shut themselves protecting themselves from the brightness and heat, I begin to get light headed as I breathe fire that will only get hotter as the flames walk near me.

Then it finally hits me. The bad guys were right.

My whole life I have done nothing but repented for my wrong doings. Not just the death of my mother, but also every bad thing I've done since then. Instead of accepting the fact that I'll make faults, like most people, I have done nothing but worry and try to be the perfect person and convince myself that I'm not as bad as Yeval and I think. I couldn't enjoy the gifts I received because I wasted so much time asking myself why. Why? 'Why does Caroline love a douche-bag like me?' for instance. I should have just held on to the gift and enjoyed it without question or debate.

So why not just live? Learn from your mistakes, instead of dwelling on them. Every second counts. And I wasted too must time repenting my sins rather than simply avoiding them in the future. There is no way for my mother to come back, there is no way for Ryan to become normal, and there is no way I can turn back time. I did the best I could and I should have been proud of how concerned I was with others, and not with myself. It didn't take years of being haunted by Yeval, or the expensive counseling, or losing my front tooth, or even losing my toe to figure this out, no; it took being stranded in a room with two dead killers that will finally be revealed as accomplices to the Slayer killings for me to figure this out. And though this fact is pathetic, I'm not going to dwell on it like I usually would. I have myself to save, and I won't quit until my heart stops beating.

I spend about a minute trying to pull the pipe, and pull my hand through the cuffs. It doesn't work. Even on a good day, I wouldn't be able to escape. I am stuck.

Breathing hurts. My head feels light. I can't see. Is the room spinning? I pass out.

Then there's pain. A pain that suddenly hits me. Am I on fire? No. It's my hand...*just* my hand. I scream. I open my eyes and see blood all over the pipe I was cuffed to, and that wall that stands behind it. I see a figure that I make out as Chief Milton, wrapping my right arm around his shoulder and picking me up. I am too weak to walk.

"Come on, kid," he says. "You have to help me on this. I'm not strong enough to carry you out." And with that, I make an attempt to walk. It seems like a lifetime before I feel the fresh air of outside.

In exhaustion, Chief lays me down on the grass that's brown from being dehydrated by the summer sun. I lay with my head up and can see the sun. It looks the same way it did when my mother died. It's funny that almost twenty years later, I am in the same position—helpless, close to my last breath, staring into the eye of the big red summer. This time I'm breathing fire from my lungs instead of water. Shit, I can't trust anything.

Caroline lays down next to me and looks me in the eyes. Her head blocks the sun from my burning eyes. The gold glow makes Caroline look like she has a halo. I knew she was an angel. She kisses and hugs me. I wrap my right arm around her and run my fingers through her blond hair. I try to take her hand with my left, but I can't. I look down and I notice it isn't there. The Chief cut my hand off.

Blood drips from it like a running facet. Chief, kneeling down next to me shirtless, puts pressure with his uniform on my handless wrist. Blood quickly soaks through.

"The ambulance is on its way," Chief reassures me.

I smile back in thanks.

Neighbors begin to gather as the three of us sit in silence and watch the warehouse flare itself into a landmark of black smoke. Its black smoke rises higher and higher, thicker and thicker, over the skies of West Seattle.

It takes the ambulance at least five minutes to arrive. The paramedics take Caroline away. She begs them to let her go with me, struggling to resist their aid.

They lift me onto a stretcher and wheel me away into the ambulance. This looks familiar. Caroline refuses to go with her own ambulance, just as I had resisted the paramedics at Alki Beach with my mother. As I am lifted into the ambulance I envision myself as I saw my mother being lifted into the ambulance. It was the last time I saw her and that's not how I want Caroline to last see me. I look down and see my arms are white. I'm dying.

The warehouse collapses before they close the ambulance door.

This is going to be all over the news tonight.

The paramedics stitch my wrist. My vision begins to fade black.

"I can't see."

I don't hear a response. I don't hear anything.

Am I passing out? Am I dying?

CHAPTER 31

# Peace

Today is the first day of the rest of my life. As is everyday. Today could possibly be the last day of my life. As could everyday. So I'm just going to live. One day will not be more special than any other. Everyday will be a good day to be alive. Yesterday is gone, today is here, and tomorrow may never come.

It's been three weeks since I lost my hand. The world declared me a hero. I refused the honor unless Chief Harold Milton could share it with me. I made an effort to decline interviews unless Milton was discussed and recognized during it. I don't know why the media wants me over Chief. He's the reason I'm alive. Maybe it's because he's a cop and I'm not. Or maybe it's just something as shallow as looks.

Eva Thomson did a twenty-minute special on Chief and I, after they had a week to whip up an hour long special on the Seattle Slayer. Eva even talked to her publisher about me. Her publisher, Mr. Jacob Anderson, read my novel (which I finished, by the way) and liked it. Though he's not interested in publishing fantasy, he likes my style of writing. He wants me to write a nonfiction novel about my experiences through the slayings. I accepted and have already written ten-thousand words. We'll see what happens.

Today at the Hermit Lounge Café, eight different people came up to me and shook my hand. Only two of them tried to have a conversation with me. Though it makes me feel good that I have made all these people feel safe on their own streets again, being unable to enjoy a hot meal with my loved ones without being interrupted is kind of gloomy.

I moved back into Caroline's apartment. Jane, her daughter, and I get along great, and Caroline thinks it's good that Jane has a father figure around. I almost beat the shit out of Jane's father with my stub-wrist over a confrontation so stupid, I can't even remember. But I decided to be the bigger man and walk away. As much as I'd like to fuck him up (it'd be easy, even with one hand), there is no need for violence unless you're defending yourself.

For money, I am getting paid for janitorial work at Chief's police station. I'm still in training, but I get paid $12.50 for the first six months. It's not great, but it's not bad.

The police station is all too familiar. During after-hours, I often clean Lime and Curtis's old office. Chief told me that once Curtis died, the entire office was stripped and reset for new detectives within a week. I often sit where Lime used to sit and think about my mother.

I wonder if there is a life after death. If there is, I imagine Lime and my mother drinking coffee and sharing good memories of me. I hope they don't blame me for their deaths, because I look back and I realize that nothing I did to them was intentional. And if they loved me like I thought they both genuinely did, I don't think I have anything to worry about.

Right now, I sit at a Detective Harmony Presley's desk. It's where Lime used to sit. My mind wanders off. I wonder if physical therapy is really helping, or if Caroline will ever find me repulsive. I almost automatically ease my fears by reminding myself that I will always try to better myself, but what happens, happens. And as long as I try to do good, there's not much else I can worry about. What's the point of living if you're just going to worry all the time?

"You're right, there is no point," says Yeval, whom I haven't seen since the day of the warehouse. "You're finally seeing life for what it is, Randy."

He sits in the chair at the desk where Curtis's used to be.

"What are you doing here?" I ask. "Curtis is dead."

"You created me yourself, Randy," he says. "You must make me go away."

"If I could, your ass would've been grass years ago," I say.

Yeval chuckles. "Listen," he says. "I have something you should see. Grab the Pearl."

"No way," I say. "Those days of the Dark Room, the Pearl, and all that other bullshit are over."

"You haven't learned everything, Randy," he tells me.

The Pearl floats between the two desks. I stand up and walk toward it.

"Where are you going to take me?" I ask.

"Same place you've always gone," he says. "Your mind."

The son of a bitch is right. It has always been in my mind…to some degree. I'm going to see what he has to show me. I grab hold of the Pearl, and am taken into the Dark Room…but it's not dark.

The Dark Room has lightened up. What always seemed like a room without light in the evening, seems now like a room lit by the sun, and as I look out the window, I see that that's what is indeed lighting the room.

The window to the right of the yellow chair is open. The woman in the orange polka-dot dress is standing and watching unicorns with a man. I walk over to the other window and see steam rise from the gravel road as usual. The dead tree is still rotting away. I try to push the window open, but it is still locked.

"That place is not for you, Randy," Yeval tells me, sitting in the same chair as he has always sat. "You can go out the other window, like you always wanted to."

Looking out of the window, I see that the ground's long golden grass is level to the floor in the Dark Room. I grab on to the window ledge for balance as I lift each foot out the window.

I still have my left hand.

I hop onto the ground. I run my fingers through golden grass. The meadow is soft but strong. The cool wind breezes through, gleaming the gold grass. I pick one out from the ground and look at it shine.

I walk several yards before I approach the man and woman in the fields. As I draw near, the man shakes the woman's hand and walks off into the deep fields and over the hills.

I approach the woman. As I walk closer, I realize what I always assumed. That woman is my mother.

"Mom!" I say.

"Hello honey," she says. "You've grown up to be a handsome man."

"I missed you so much," I say, grabbing her and hugging her tight.

I break into tears.

After minutes of holding each other, she says, "I've missed you more."

"Mom, I'm a screw up," I confess to her. "I've abused myself, gotten myself into so much trouble, hurt the ones I've loved and no matter what, I just can't move on."

"But you have to, Randy," she says. "You are going to hurt the ones you love again too. It's just the way the world works. Life is beautiful and ugly. You have to accept and live with both. You can't pass the beautiful by just in order to avoid the ugly, Randy. That is a waste of life. You have to roll with the punches. Do as I did, and live every moment with happiness. Even during the sad times. Try to make good decisions, and when you do make the bad ones, which you will, learn from them, don't dwell on them."

"I'm just having a hard time trying to look away from the ugliness in the world," I say. "It's everywhere I go. In my mind, on the news, everywhere. It's like I can't escape it."

"You've been through a lot, and it will take a while for you adjust," she says. "But you have to try, and you have to accept set backs. You can't let the world you live in make life seem so ugly. Be fortunate for what you have, and don't be angry for the things you don't. Most importantly, be happy that you're alive and make the most of it. Your life might be over during your happiest moment.

"Take me for example. It was a beautiful day. I was at the beach with the love of my life and I was pregnant with another gift. Before I knew it, you were sucked out into the water, my unborn child was injured, and I was dying on the beach. It all ended in fear and pain for me. But it did have a happy ending."

"What! How?" I ask angrily. "You know how depressed I have been all these years."

"It ended happily because you and Ryan are still alive. I would rather be dead and have both of you alive. All three of us could've been dead that day, but only one of us died. And it was the only one of the three I would choose to die. I wish it didn't happen, but I still had something to be grateful about. And I have to accept the fact that that did happen."

"You're right," I say.

"You learned a lot through all these years of pain and depression, Randy," she says. "Don't think it all went to waste. You have come to the point where you have realized what is what."

"Wait a minute," I say. "You are all in my imagination? You are all in my mind?"

"Yes, Randy," she says. "You finally came to the point in your life where you are able to realize what you want out of it. You sorted everything out for yourself. You made use of your pain.

"Some people don't even think as deep as you are right now," she continues. Some people think deeply in different ways. Some people don't do much thinking at all."

"Yeah, I can name a few people like that," I say.

"What matters is that you are able to cope with what happened. It will be painful, but you've realized that I am not coming back and that there is nothing you can do to change that.

"Now, stop dwelling on the past and go live. Live for me. Live for what I died for. Be everything you can be. Take care of your brother, he is your best friend. Be good to your father, he's half the reason you are here. Treat Caroline right, you know she's the one you want; a lot of people aren't lucky enough to know that kind of love. Be happy for what you have."

"Okay," I say.

She opens her arms to me.

"Randy, I may be part of your imagination," she begins, "but I am always here with you. I have never left you. I may not be with you in this life, but I am watching over you someplace else."

As I hold her tight, I ask her, "Where are you watching me from, Mom?"

"You'll know," she whispers softly, the same way she used to whisper to me in my crib. "And the day you know is the day we'll be together again."

She lets go of me. Looking me in the eye, she smiles at me and then turns away. She walks over the hill and into the distance.

I take my time walking back to the Dark Room. It looks like a small lodge from the outside, about to collapse. With every step I take on the way back, I think of how much I have to live for. I also cherish all the good times I had.

I climb back in the Dark Room and see Yeval still sitting in the chair. He holds his palm out and reveals the ruby lying in it.

"You ready?" he asks me.

"Yes, I am," I say, taking the ruby.

I wake up in the chair at the desk. How long have I been out?

"Hey, you done with everything?" my boss, Mr. Martin, asks me.

"Everything is just beginning," I say.

"What?" he asks, because he didn't hear me.

"Almost, sir," I say.

Mr. Martin nods his head and walks off.

"Goodbye, Randy," Yeval says. He is still sitting in the same chair.

"I wish I knew what to say, Yeval," I tell him. What do I say? Bon voyage? Nice to know you? Thanks for all the years of guilt? I forgive you? I'll miss you…in a way?

"All of the above," he says.

"What?"

"Remember, I'm in your mind," he says.

He winks at me and we laugh together.

For the first time, Yeval doesn't leave in a vanish. He slowly dissolves into the air.

There is complete silence. I feel different. As if I can think to myself in tranquility. Nothing moves. I sit in the dark office alone. I unplug the heater, humming away and the only thing I can hear now is myself breathing and my heart pumping. Complete silence. Yeval is gone and I can now think.

There is peace.

## CHAPTER 32

# Life

Life is good. Life is good when you wake up in the middle of the night and see the person you've been dreaming about sleeping next to you. You really know you have found happiness when you're pushing thirty and you don't have any needs or wishes. You really know you have found happiness when the only thing you can bitch about is having to wake up to start work at 5am. Yes, I guess life is pretty good.

I give myself a thwarted look in the mirror as I finish dressing up for work. Mr. Martin requires me to wear faded blue jeans and black or brown tennis shoes (my Jordans). I was given a grey button up shirt with my name sewn into the left breast. They also want me to comb my hair. I don't mind being a janitor and all, but it just doesn't make sense to have someone who is cleaning up filth look presentable. It's a Goddamn dirty job.

I decide to take the elevator in my apartment complex this morning because I'm running a bit late. Knowing Seattle's traffic, I'll probably be late. I usually take the stairs to get the blood flowing and the muscles moving, but today is an exception.

From time to time I feel depressed and embarrassed of having only one hand. A lot of people look at me as a hero, others look at me as a freak. My faint limp is a give away that I'm missing a toe. At least I got a front tooth implanted.

On the fifteen second wait inside the elevator, I don't do much but obsess about my hand. But, I shouldn't complain. It was either my hand or burning to death.

The elevator door opens and there is the biggest coincidence...there is a burn victim approaching the elevator. He carries with him a suit case. I wonder if he is just coming home from work. I wonder if he works a night job just to avoid people looking like him.

When I first see him, there is a twitch in my stomach. It's like I saw a monster. Then when I absorb the fact that he's a victim of a fire, as I almost was, I give him the courtesy of looking him right in the eye.

As he passes me, I smile at him and say, "Good morning."

When he looks at me, he is at first taken aback. I don't know if I startled him or what, but he sure looks nervous. Perhaps, he's not used to this much attention.

"Good morning," he replies, lowering his voice.

"Have a nice day," I say as I walk into the garage and the elevator door closes with him inside.

At work, while sweeping the bathroom floor, I think about what the burnt man has to live for. If he were to backpack through Europe or cruise the small islands in the Pacific, he could never escape people staring at him or looking away. Shit, even people look at me with pity in their eyes—I can't even imagine what they must do to him.

It is Tuesday morning. Caroline, my father, and I will go over to Ryan's to watch movies like we do every Tuesday. Last week they actually had the residents watch *Casablanca*. I like the movie, but I was amazed at how residents were actually sucked into the story.

Tuesday is the day for the four of us to hang out. Friday morning is the day we all have breakfast. Not everybody has people who love them like me. I feel really lucky.

The floor is almost sparkling clean when some deputy comes in to take a shit and completely ruin my hard work. I almost want to harass him while shit plops in the toilet. "Ooh, that sounded like a big one," or "Jesus, what'd you eat?" are what I'd say if I had nothing to lose.

The deputy takes a ten minute shit, though he actually just stalls for another good five minutes so he doesn't have to work. He leaves, doesn't wash his hands, and I am alone again.

I look at myself in the mirror and try to make peace with who I am.

"This is who you are," I say to myself out loud. "This is how the world sees you. Don't let them know your pain."

I clearly remember how I looked as a child. My hair was actually thin and straight, not thick and wavy as it has become. My white teeth so tiny for my big smile have fallen out and grown in too large. I wonder how Caroline, Morgan, Jenkins's secretary, and all the other women find that smile of mine attractive. The fake tooth looks real. My bright blue eyes have gone darker. I have changed so much, and I will change even more. This is what I look like, and it's how the world sees me. I'm a handsome man with demons I can't face. The world doesn't see that, and they might not even care.

I grip the sink I cleaned just minutes ago, and put my face close to the mirror. I look into my own eyes and try to see and possibly understand all the pain I have endured during my short time on Earth. There is no telling what pain the future holds. But, there is no pleasure or beauty without pain, as my mother would say. It's time to move on. Moving on is every second. The present is just a trail that I am walking on—the past blew away with the wind, and the future is the only path I can take.

I suddenly hear the sound of the triangle. I look around the bathroom. I'm looking, but I see nothing. I get down on my knees and look under the sink. No Yeval. No Pearl. I push open each and every stall. Nothing. For a moment, out of the corner of my eye, I think I see Yeval. But the red figure disappears as I turn to look.

Whatever I saw, it was standing by the corner that blocks the door. I walk around the corner and see nothing but the bathroom door. I hear someone approach. The door opens. It's Chief Milton.

"Working hard, friend?" Chief says as he walks around the corner and heads to one of the urinals.

"Just got done beating off," I say. "Now I'm gonna start working."

Chief unzips and takes a leak. It takes him a while to get going, and when he's done I have to remind him to zip his fly. He's washing his hands, when I notice a concerned look on his face.

"What is it, Chief?"

"Huh?"

"Something's on your mind."

"No. It's nothing. Really, it's nothing."

"You sure?" I ask. "The look in your eyes tells me it ain't nothing."

He turns off the facet, wipes his hands with some paper towels and throws them in the garbage can, frustrated.

"Listen," he begins. "I gotta tell you something that you can't tell anybody else."

"Shoot," I say, fully confident that I am ready for whatever Chief is about to say.

"I also need you to promise me you won't get upset."

"I'll be fine," I reassure him.

"Are you sure? I know how you can't get."

"I'll be fine," I repeat.

"Well, you know that warehouse?" he asks.

"The one that caught fire?" I ask.

"Yeah," he says.

"Yes, of course," I say. "Why?"

"Everything has been cleaned up, right?" he says. "Well, I just got word that they only found one body."

"What?"

I'd rather get kicked in the balls than hear what I just heard.

"They only found one body," he says. "But don't worry, it's probably nothing. The other's remains will probably turn up."

"It can't be. I watched both of them die," I say, very distressed.

I start twitching and breathing deeply. The ground under my feet has just been lifted.

"You promised me you wouldn't get upset, Randy."

"You were there. You saw them die. Nobody could survive that."

"Well, I only saw Jenkins die," he says. "And, yes, nobody would be able to escape that fire. Not without being badly burned."

I drop the mop and run out of the bathroom. I make my twenty minute drive home from work in only five minutes. I cut every stop sign and red light and don't drop below 40 mph until I reach the apartment. I run up the stairs and inside.

I turn the knob. It's unlocked.

"I wouldn't go in there if I were you," I hear a voice. I turn around to see who it is. It's Yeval.

"I thought you were gone," I say. "Gone with Curtis."

Then it hits me. Yeval is still here because Curtis is still alive. Or is he?

"Who said Curtis died?" says Yeval, smiling.

"Nobody," I say. "Why? Did he?"

"I'm not telling," he says, breaking a laugh.

"Fuck you," I say, pushing the door open and entering.

"Keep this in mind though, Randy," Yeval says. "If you and Curtis can both coincidentally create me over obsessive guilt, isn't it possible someone else who is also constantly living with guilt create me?"

I ignore him and enter. The living room looks untouched.

"Caroline? Jane?" I call out. There is no answer.

I walk to our bedroom and see an envelope on my bed. I open it up and a picture falls out. It is a picture of Caroline, Jane and Ryan tied together on a couch, their mouths taped shut.

My first thought is to immediately call the police. But then I realize that Yeval/Curtis would also go after my father too. So, I call my father first. The phone rings several times and his answering machine picks up: "Hi this is Kenneth. Leave me a message and I'll get back to you."

I am about to leave a message, but then I realize that my father would've picked up if he was okay. So I hang up and call the police.

"911 emergency," says the operator.

"Yes, I need the police to come to 19677 California Ave. SW immediately."

"What's the problem, sir?"

"It's a fucking emergency," I scream into the phone and then hang up.

My cell phone rings. I look at the incoming call. It says, "Asshole". I forgot to change the name from "Asshole" to "Dad" after him and I made up.

"Dad," I say, picking up the phone. "Listen, if you're at home, get out and head to my place. Ryan, Caroline and Jane have been kidnapped."

There is no response.

"Hello?" I say again.

After a couple of seconds I hear the faint sound of breathing. Then a voice, that I can't tell if I know or not, whispers clearly into the phone, "Slayer."